Skylar Robbins
The MYSTERY of SHADOW HILLS

Carrie Cross

TEEN
MYSTERY
PRESS

Skylar Robbins: The Mystery of Shadow Hills
by Carrie Cross

ISBN:
978-0-9894143-0-2 (print)
978-0-9894143-1-9 (ebook)

LCCN:
2013945188

Cover design: Ed Ward
www.mentalwarddesign.net

For my mom

ACKNOWLEDGEMENTS

A heartfelt thank you to my parents, Sylvia and Jim Cross, and my wonderful husband Ed, for their tireless support, excellent constructive criticism, and Ed for my awesome cover. Thank you to my close friend, author Elayne Angel, for her amazing, astute edits and creative suggestions. This book would not be the same without their input.

Thanks to Beth Lieberman Editorial for her critiques and advice, and my friends and family for their suggestions and constant encouragement: Laura and Barbara Riddle, Cara Tadman, Carolyn Marshall Conduris, Cammy Grajek, Holli Walker, Jill Paschke, Kraig and Lisa Kelly, Molly Johnson, Kevin and Patti Beechum, Rebecca Soborro, Kim Ortiz, Ray Burke and the rest of the Beech gang; my extended family, and my Top Secret Sister, Rachel Slaughter.

And thank you to these former and present middle graders for giving me a look inside middle school today and for their reviews: Sara Epstein, Kristin Wypiszynski, Tara the Tiger Nyman, Kyler Brodzinski, Erin Ryan, Aaliyah Murphy, Hannah Rose Dickinson, Chloe Drehmer, and Kelsey Garcia.

Contents

Skylar Robbins
The MYSTERY of SHADOW HILLS

1
My Detective Kit

Heading for Malibu on a sunny Saturday in June would normally have been a good thing. I could have spent the day bodysurfing with my BFF, Alexa, and playing games in the arcade on the Santa Monica pier. If I was totally lucky I might have shared a bumper car with Dustin Coles, the cutest boy going into Pacific Middle School. Alexa and I liked to lie in the sun and watch surfers ride the waves on Zuma beach. If there were pinball and corndogs ahead of me instead of what I was in for, I would have begged my dad for a ride down the coast. But today? Not so much.

If I'd gotten out of the car right then and spread out my beach towel, everything might have turned out fine. But my dad kept right on driving.

We stopped at a red light before heading down the incline to Pacific Coast Highway. Comforted a little by the weight pressing against my leg, I stared out the window and watched the ocean. The faraway water was navy blue where it met the sky. A frosting of whitecaps drifted sideways, winked, and disappeared. The sea was teal-blue in the middle, and the shallow water glowed bright green as if it were lit from below. Small waves welled up, and then the whitewater bubbled forward and sizzled flat on the sand.

Thin sunlight shimmered on the ocean while I tapped my fingers on the detective kit leaning against my leg. I'd always wanted to become a private detective like my grandfather, and used his old leather briefcase to hold my tools. Back when he was a policeman, Grandpa's case used to be a rich tan color. But after decades of visiting crime scenes, sitting outside in the sun, and baking in a hot cop car, it had faded to grayish beige. There was a burn mark on the bottom from when he'd policed an arson scene. The handle was stained with dark smudges from dusting robbery sites with fingerprinting powder. After he went undercover, the corners got battered from years of being tossed into the trunk of his unmarked car.

I had been adding to my detective kit slowly over the last two years by using my allowance and asking for pieces of equipment for my birthday. The first pocket hid a thin penlight that I used for searching through boxes, suitcases, or suspicious people's belongings in the dark. Another one held a laser pointer that shot a red beam of light up to a hundred yards. My mom always worried that I would blind myself or someone else with it, but I kept it in case I was ever chased by robbers or someone I needed to blind to save my life. My pink Super-Zoom binoculars, perfect for long-distance spying, rested inside the biggest pocket. A heavy-duty flashlight for nighttime investigations was snug under a strap.

Zipped inside another compartment there was a measuring tape, wax for taking impressions, and a box of chalk in case I had to outline a dead body. I had a pen and sketchpad for describing crime scenes, a magnifying glass, and tweezers and evidence envelopes for picking up and storing clues. There were latex gloves like doctors use, and safety goggles. Pepper spray for self-defense. Best of all was my fingerprinting kit and Case Solution cards for mounting the prints.

I loved my detective kit and everything it stood for. Where I was headed, there was no way I was leaving it behind. *Uh-uh.* Not today.

The light changed, and we turned onto Pacific Coast Highway and passed the Santa Monica pier. The Ferris wheel spun lazily around, carrying happy people toward the sky. The pink chair at the top of the wheel swung back and forth, empty. I always felt lucky when it was my turn to get on the ride and a pink car stopped in front of me. I didn't feel lucky today. Wishing I were waiting in line for that ride right now, I looked out the back window and watched the Ferris wheel turn until I couldn't see it any longer.

A few miles farther up the coast, my mom pointed at a mansion built high up on a cliff. "Look, Honey," she said to me. The huge house had a wall of windows that faced the ocean. A black Ferrari was parked in the driveway, and a modern metal sculpture dominated the yard. "I bet a movie star lives there. Or a rock star." She smiled at me over her shoulder. "Maybe that's Justin Bieber's house."

My mom didn't watch *Extra*, read *People* magazine, or download music from iTunes. If it wasn't in a textbook, she usually didn't have a clue. "He lives in Hollywood Hills, Mom." My detective kit tipped over when we stopped for a light and I bent sideways to grab the handle and straighten it back up.

"Just because someone can afford a house like that doesn't mean he's famous," my dad said. "Maybe a chemist owns it, for example." He winked at me in the rearview mirror and his blue eyes crinkled behind his glasses.

Ha ha. My dad's a chemist. As if we could ever afford a huge beach house. "What do you think, Skylar? Who lives there?" he asked, trying to start one of our old car games like I was a fussy six-year-old.

"Mickey and his roommate Donald?" I stared out the window at the roiling ocean. "I still can't believe I have to spend the whole summer with Gwendolyn. You know how she is," I complained, picking at a thread on the seatbelt. My cousin and I did not get along. And that was the understatement of the century.

"Gwendolyn acts out because she has low self-esteem," my mom told me for the millionth time. Like that made it OK.

My dad sped up when we hit a straight part of the coastline. "Just ignore her. If she doesn't get a reaction she'll get bored and leave you alone." His shoulders bunched up and he tapped his fingers quickly against the steering wheel.

"I try to ignore her. It doesn't do any good. She just gets in my face and asks me if I went deaf." I flicked the seatbelt buckle as we passed a long row of unevenly spaced palm trees.

"Gwendolyn got suspended for a week last semester for bullying that boy in her class, remember?" my dad asked. "I'm sure she'll be on her best behavior."

Gwendolyn doesn't have any best behavior, I thought.

My cousin had picked on me since we were kids. She made fun of me because I was skinny and got good grades. My mom said it just showed that my cousin wished she were thinner and did better in school. But that didn't make it feel any better when I was at the end

4

of her pointing finger. I remembered what happened two weeks ago on report card day. I got mostly *A*'s and Gwendolyn barely made *C*'s. "Gee Skylar, no wonder you don't have a boyfriend with your nose always stuck in those big, boring books," Gwendolyn said. "I don't know how you can stand to be so bo-oh-oh-ring."

After she'd said that I pulled out a small notepad that I always carry with me. I jotted a note to myself while staring at Gwendolyn with a little smile on my face: *I'm not as boring as you think.*

So then Gwendolyn whined, "What are you writing?"

I'd won that time. But she got me back after dinner.

"Hey Skylar, are you sure you're a girl?" Gwendolyn asked, bending over to stare at my flat chest. "You look like a scarecrow." She walked away, laughing and stuffing cookies into her face.

It seemed like my cousin only smiled when she was laughing at someone else. She had short, frizzy hair and a round face, and she didn't shower very often. Sometimes she would stand right next to where I was sitting and fart on purpose. Then she'd hold her nose and look at me like I did it.

"It's not all about Gwendolyn," I said. "Staying at her house also means I can't hang out with Alexa for like, *forever*." I couldn't spend the whole summer without my BFF. No way. And it would be impossible for her, too. Especially if she had to go to summer school and I wasn't there to help her.

"Maybe one Saturday Caroline can give you a ride and you can meet Alexa and her mom halfway. For lunch." My mom ran a hand through her hair, which was dark brown like mine, except hers was short and wavy while mine was long and straight.

"I don't want to 'do lunch' with Alexa, Mom. I want to be able to ride my bike over to her house and be there in five minutes. Or go swimming, or go to the mall." *Or what if we just want to hang out and spy on boys?* I thought, but didn't say. Wouldn't have helped my case.

"You'll meet all sorts of new friends at Malibu Middle School this summer," my dad said helpfully. He was trying to make me feel better, but the thought of starting a new school just made me nervous. My situation was like the next wave. It was coming whether I liked it or not, and there was nothing I could do to stop it.

My mom craned her neck around and looked at me sympathetically. "I'm sorry we couldn't take you with us, Honey, but the trip is for the professors and their spouses only. No children are coming. Plus you'd be bored silly. We're going to visit all the historical monuments I teach about in class. The Berlin Wall—" she laughed, shaking the hair away from her heart-shaped face. "Well actually where the Berlin Wall *was*…."

"It's OK, Mom," I said. Visiting the remains of the Berlin Wall sounded as exciting as a triple helping of detention. But it was still so not OK. "I just don't see why I couldn't have stayed at our house."

"We can't let you stay home alone for eight weeks, Kiddo," my dad said, scratching his head through his thin light brown hair. "You're too young."

"I'm thirteen, Dad." I fingered one of the locks on my detective kit, spinning the digits around.

"Exactly." He put his hand firmly back on the wheel.

6

"Case closed."

I stared out the window to my right. The rocky hillside was covered with dry tumbleweeds and dead bushes, some still black from last year's fires. It happened every year when everything was all dried out and the Santa Ana winds blew hot air through the hills. Sometimes a homeless person cooking outside would start a fire by accident, or some crazy person would start one on purpose. Other times the hillside seemed to burst into flames all by itself. Whenever it got windy and we were at my cousin's house, Aunt Caroline's eyes would pinch up at the corners as she squinted out the back window. She'd twist her fingers around as she listened for fire engine sirens, sniffing the air every five seconds to see if she smelled smoke.

The mountain looped and snaked with the coastline, and now there were no plants or trees on the hillside. It was just a wall of striped rock that looked impossible to climb. My parents kept trying to convince me how great my summer would be as we got closer to Gwendolyn's, which was up in the Malibu hills past Point Dume. Behind her house, a rocky mountain range stretched toward the sky. The face was covered with low bushes and big rocks, creating pockets of light and dark. Each time you looked up at the hillside it looked different. The shadows seemed to move and dance, darting and disappearing with the setting sun. They looked like caves where people or animals could hide.

The locals had nicknamed those mountains, "Shadow Hills."

2
Shadow Hills

"You have your bicycle and your detective kit," my dad reminded me. "You'll have a whole new neighborhood to investigate." Since I'm practicing to be a private detective he thought this would excite me.

"They have horses you can ride, and a huge swimming pool," my mom said. "Caroline hired a trainer so she can learn to ride side-saddle. You can take horseback riding lessons."

My stomach lurched.

I'd been making excuses to get out of riding my aunt's horses for years, so I wasn't about to admit to my parents now that taking lessons was the absolute last thing I wanted to do. I pulled out my phone and texted Alexa.

This just keeps getting worse. Horseback lessons n summer school w G.

My cell chirped a second later.

Dt wrry u wnt fal f.

My BFF had a learning disability called *dyslexia*, which made it really hard for her to read and spell. But I could usually manage to figure out her texts. *Don't worry, you won't fall off.* As in, the horse. Like I was about to climb up onto the back of one of those giant animals. I'd probably sail right over it and land on my butt on the other side. No thank you.

I texted Alexa back: **I'd rather eat someone's earwax.**

LOL. IL sav u mine.

Another wave crunched the shore. The foam was yellowish brown as it slid across the sand. It looked dirty, like it was thick with particles of rotten fish. We turned off Pacific Coast Highway and headed up the hill. As I wondered desperately if there was any way to get myself out of staying with Gwendolyn for eight weeks, we pulled up to the estate.

My cousin's driveway was so curved and steep that it looked like an Olympic skateboard ramp. After my dad said, "Hi. It's us," into a little speaker, a black iron gate opened slowly. He drove up to the house and set the parking brake. We all sat there for a second, like nobody wanted to move first. Because once someone did there would be no turning back. Then my mom and dad both reached sideways, like they'd practiced it. She opened her door and my dad popped the trunk. I sat in the car until the last possible second while my dad took my bike off the rack and lifted out my suitcase. Grabbing my backpack and my detective kit, I dragged myself out of the car. I had absolutely no choice. I followed my parents up the driveway and into Aunt Caroline and Uncle Jim's house.

We all crowded into the entryway, which was tall and narrow with a two-story high ceiling. A big skylight at the top let in dim sunshine through a sticky layer of spider webs. When my aunt shut the front door, the dirty webs flapped around up there. The air smelled stale and tight, like no one had breathed it in days. I stared at my dad's back, my fingers sweating on the handle of my detective kit.

"Caroline," my mom sang, smiling as if they hadn't seen each other in years.

"Samantha!" my aunt cried, her voice echoing up the skinny entryway. She looked nervous. This wasn't like every other visit, where my parents dropped me off and picked me up the same day, or I slept over for one night.

Aunt Caroline had the same heart-shaped face as my mom, but her hair was much shorter and frosted with highlights. The way my aunt moved her hands when she talked reminded me of baby birds fluttering around. They hugged each other and then Aunt Caroline turned to me. "You're going to have a wonderful time with us while your parents are abroad, Skylar." She put her hands on my shoulders and looked into my eyes with a sympathetic little pout on her face. Like she knew how I was feeling.

She had no idea how I was feeling.

"Come in, come in," she said, leading us out of the stuffy foyer and into the living room.

The smell of their house hit me right away: old carpet and boiled cabbage. My mom called their house "a Malibu mansion," when she talked to her friends about what a catch my uncle had been. When she spoke to my dad in private she used words like "dated," and "needs remodeling." I thought the place was pretty creepy, but it was kind of cool, too. Like there's this spiral staircase that starts in the corner of the living room and leads up to a round mirror on the ceiling. When you look up the stairs and into the mirror it looks like the staircase goes on forever. But it really leads nowhere.

There are other spooky things about the house that you wouldn't notice right away. One of them has to do with my dead Great-Aunt Evelyn, and the attic. It makes the hair stand up on my arms. Worse yet, there's a rumor that people do wicked things up in the hills at night. A trail leading into Shadow Hills starts a little way past a row of pines at the end of the backyard. You could see those trees through the kitchen windows, if you wanted to.

My uncle walked in and set down his briefcase. Uncle Jim was still in his business suit but he'd loosened his tie. He was an entertainment lawyer, so sometimes he had to meet clients on Saturdays. When he turned to talk to my dad I saw the shiny bald circle on the back of my uncle's head. My cousin slouched against a dark wall between two huge paintings, eating ruffled potato chips out of a jumbo-sized bag. Gwendolyn scraped potato off a back tooth with one finger, examined the morsel, and ate it. "You've had enough chips, Gwendolyn," my aunt told her.

"OK," my cousin said pleasantly. She tipped her head back and poured the last few crumbs into her mouth, then crumpled up the empty bag. "Pick your room carefully," Gwendolyn warned me. "Hope you're not afraid of the dark." She let out a cackle and left the room.

My mom glanced at my dad and then they both turned toward me. I gave them a look like, *"See what you're doing to me?"*

Aunt Caroline called after my cousin's back. "Subtle threats? No bullying, Gwendolyn, remember? Consequences," she hinted.

Gwendolyn shrugged as she turned a corner. The dark hallway swallowed her up like a frog gulping down a chubby fly. She knew there would be no consequences.

My dad leaned into me and talked softly, as if no one would notice. "Bullies thrive on making people angry. Don't let her get to you." Then he ruffled my hair like I was four years old. I looked at my feet, brushing my pink sneaker over a stain on the carpet.

"Pay no attention to Gwendolyn," Aunt Caroline told me. "There's nothing wrong with any of the bedrooms. Let's go pick out yours."

"Go ahead, Honey," my mom said. Then she and my uncle started discussing curfews, check-in times, and house rules. If my aunt was anything like my mom, I was sure to get a written list.

Looking past the living room and out the kitchen windows, I saw the mountains stretching up behind the end of the long backyard. The sun was overhead, and Shadow Hills looked shiny and bright in spots, shaded and dark in others.

I followed Aunt Caroline up the stairs to the second floor and down a narrow hallway. We passed a row of cave-shaped nooks that held ugly knickknacks. My aunt showed me two of the guest rooms, and they were both dark and kind of creepy. The first one looked old-fashioned. Its pale bedspread was printed with dainty flowers, and the little table in front of a framed mirror was wrapped in a heavy skirt. On the shelves, thick boring books were layered with dust. The windows were tiny and too high up to look out of.

I shook my head.

"Gwendolyn's room is at the end of the hall, so if you want to be near her, you might like this one." Aunt Caroline turned a corner and opened the next door. I looked into a gloomy room with dark wood paneling, maroon curtains, and a brown bedspread. An ancient floor lamp stood in the corner. A thick spider web with a bug stuck in the middle of it spread from the shade to the post. Next to the lamp, a wooden chair with stick legs held a thin cushion. There was a painting on the wall of a stern farmer holding a pitchfork. He glared at me. Not only was the room awful, but I wanted to be as far away from Gwendolyn as possible.

"I'm sorry," I said.

"Or there's the rose room, but I'm afraid it's kind of small." We walked down another hall, my aunt opened a door, and I knew I'd found my room.

This bedroom was narrow, with a slanted wood beam ceiling that was real high on one side and sloped down sharply to meet the opposite wall. The bedspread and pillow covers were patterned with wild roses. Their swirling dark green vines matched the color of the carpet. At the end of the room there was a cozy alcove with a cushioned window seat. Its bay window opened to a twisted oak tree growing right outside. I thought it would be a perfect place to start writing a mystery story while I waited for the summer to be over. I could call it, "Trapped in Malibu: No Way Out." It would star a junior detective who had just turned thirteen, and had brown hair and dark blue eyes, like mine.

"I like this room," I said, and Aunt Caroline smiled.

We walked out of the bedroom and turned a corner, passing a narrow door that my cousin said hid a steep staircase. The hidden staircase led up to the attic. I had never been up those stairs, even when Gwendolyn dared me.

"You know the rule, right?" my aunt asked, and I shrugged.

"Stay out of the attic. Please." Then the smile dropped off her face. "More importantly, Shadow Hills are off limits. Especially after dark."

3
Dead Aunt Evelyn's "Things"

L ike I'd want to explore the creepy hillside in the middle of the night. Forget about the hills, I wanted to walk straight up those stairs and find out what she was hiding in the attic. "What's wrong with the attic?" I asked. "Not that I want to go inside it. Just curious."

Aunt Caroline looked away, flicking imaginary dust off the end of the banister. I could tell she was stalling while she tried to think up an excuse. "My Aunt Evelyn's things are in the attic, and it's messy and dusty. You're welcome to explore anywhere else in the entire house or on the grounds. Except for the pool and the stable unless there is an adult present." She smiled nicely, but I wasn't convinced. I knew the real reason I wasn't allowed in the attic: Gwendolyn told me that our dead great-aunt's ashes had been up there in their urn, and they'd spilled. That's what Aunt Evelyn's "things" really were. *Gross.*

"I'll tell Jim you chose the rose room and he can bring up your suitcase." On our way back through the halls we passed a light flickering behind a green lampshade and a painting of a clown wearing a tattered plaid suit. Then we headed down the stairs.

We crossed through the big living room and walked into the entryway, and then it was time to say goodbye. The moment I'd been dreading most of all had finally come. My dad hugged me really hard, and then it was my mom's turn. She held me tight and whispered, "I'm sorry," in my ear while I inhaled a last trace of her perfume. I still couldn't believe they had chosen Europe over me, and watched them walk down the driveway with tears filling my eyes. The sound of my dad's car starting sealed it. They were really leaving me. Far away from my friends, stuck at a new school, in the same house with Gwendolyn. For eight weeks.

My mom looked at me over her shoulder while their car moved slowly down my cousin's driveway and her face crumpled. Then she turned around and all I could see was the backs of my parents' heads, their bumper, and spinning tires. And they were gone.

Walking back through a maze of hallways to my slanted room, my throat ached from trying not to cry. I didn't want to give my cousin something else to make fun of. I could just imagine her singing out, "Sky-lar is a *cry ba-by!*" as I closed the door.

I sat down on the rose-patterned cushion in the alcove, rested my forehead against the window, and finally let it out. As tears rolled down my cheeks, I looked through the oak tree branches into the backyard below, wondering how I would keep from going crazy. Hoping to catch a glimpse of the ocean, I looked past the edge of the yard where it dropped off down the hillside. But beyond that there was just a valley filled with fog. It looked like a giant bowl of clouds, floating and lost.

I reached toward the bedside stand, groping for my diary. Writing about my problems usually made me feel better. But I hadn't unpacked yet, and my diary wasn't there. Besides, writing about my situation wouldn't make it suck any less. I was stuck in this Malibu nightmare. For now.

Hugging my knees, I squished my eyes against them, forcing the tears away. There was nothing I could do about my situation yet, but I would come up with a plan to get myself out of this house. No way was I staying here for eight whole weeks. I would escape from Malibu! While my mom and dad paraded around Europe touring historical monuments and museums, I would stow away on an airplane and fly to somewhere much more exciting, leaving my grouchy cousin behind. Moments later I was lost in my favorite daydream. The one where I was an undercover detective, traveling the world on Top Secret missions. I could see it now:

My First Class airplane seat was as wide as my dad's recliner and twice as comfy. I wore a gray wig pulled back in a bun, and granny glasses hid my eyes. A pretty flight attendant bent forward and offered me a glass of champagne, but I brushed it away. I had to keep my head clear and my mind sharp. Someone was smuggling millions of dollars worth of counterfeit money into Costa Rica and pumping it into a casino. So far, neither the FBI nor the CIA had been able to catch the criminal.

Skylar Robbins: Teen Detective stepped up to the plate.

I'd searched the Internet for someone who bought plane tickets to Costa Rica each time the phony money appeared and the casino made a big bank deposit. Checking names against dates, in seconds I found an exact match.

That smuggler occupied the seat right behind mine. As day turned into night, the cabin darkened and the thief behind me began to snore. Carefully removing a set of plastic handcuffs from my carry-on bag, I crept out of my seat. Before she knew she was busted I had them clamped around her wrists.

I shook off the fantasy and decided I might as well unpack—but just a few things since I knew I'd be leaving soon to start a new adventure. First I took my diary out of my suitcase and looked around for a good place to hide it. I knew Gwendolyn would figure out all the easy hiding spots really fast. Opening the narrow closet door, I pulled on a cord that dangled from the ceiling, lighting a dim bulb. There were some shiny black hatboxes stacked in the corner. The one on top was covered with dust and held a felt hat decorated with pink ribbon. The hat inside the second box had a burgundy plume that filled up the whole space. I slipped my diary under a cowboy hat in the third box down and set the other hatboxes on top of it. I knew it was a lame hiding place, but it would have to do for now.

Then I turned back to the other things I'd brought from home. First, I pulled my detective kit out from under the bed. It just fit underneath, lying on its side. I used at least one item from my kit almost every day, so there's no way I was leaving it at home.

I fingered the locks. An amateur detective would use a combination that was simple to remember, like their birthday. But my grandfather taught me that this was the easiest code to crack. The hardest combination to guess was one that was totally random. But I also had to be able to remember it, and open it at a moment's notice without a decoder key. So for this I used a plain code, where each letter of the alphabet had a number: A = 1, B = 2, like that. Then I translated a word into numbers: 6-2-9.

My grandfather's face popped into my mind, and

within seconds I was longing to see him again. Grandpa had taught me all sorts of important skills for finding clues, investigating mysteries, and solving cases. I remembered how he taught me to lift fingerprints like it was yesterday:

Grandpa treated me to a blue-eyed smile. Then he winked at me and held out his hand with a Kleenex covering his palm. "Let's see that juice box." I put the box of Juicy-Juice I'd just finished on the tissue. He moved it onto the table in front of him, careful not to touch the surfaces of the box with his fingers. "This is fingerprinting powder," he explained, holding up what looked like a jar of dark ash. "Watch," my grandfather said, sprinkling some of the powder onto the side of the juice box. Then he took a big soft brush and whisked most of the powder onto a napkin.

I leaned closer. A crisp, gray copy of my fingerprint stuck to the side of the waxy box like a decal on the back of my bike.

"Now we lift the print." Grandpa removed a clear, sticky piece of tape from a roll. He pressed it down on top of my fingerprint, and then very slowly peeled the tape off of the box. "See?" he said, showing it to me. My fingerprint made a perfect picture on the clear tape. "Now let's mount this on a Case Solution card." He took a card off the stack he had in his detective kit, and pressed the tape down onto the card, trapping my print. I watched him fill in the case line. Since there was no case number he just wrote, Skylar's fingerprint.

Grandpa handed me the card. "It's yours to keep. Next weekend we'll print someone else and I'll teach you how to compare fingerprints to see if you can find a match."

Case Solution:
Skylar's fingerprint

"OK," I said, wrapping my arms around his neck. "Let's print Mom."

"Let's," he agreed, his eyes full of fun.

Looking at my detective kit really made me miss my grandfather. I closed the lid, scrambled the numbers on the combination locks, and stashed my kit under the bed. Then I looked around the small room, wondering what to do next.

An oval mirror in a heavy frame hung on the wall next to the alcove, and I looked into it. My round blue eyes were bloodshot, and my nose and cheeks looked pink beneath the freckles. My hair needed brushing but I didn't bother. Picturing Gwendolyn annoying me all summer and our Great-Aunt Evelyn's "things" dusting the attic, suddenly I had to get outside into the fresh air.

I ran down the stairs, through the kitchen, and out the sliding glass door into the backyard. The cool ocean air smelled of salt and fish, like wet seashells. Behind the house, the left side of the yard was woodsy and crowded with weeping willows and evergreens. Gwendolyn liked to brag that her backyard was so big she didn't even know exactly where it ended. A skinny stream trickled between the trees, disappearing down the hill on the far left side of the estate.

The middle of the yard had a swimming pool, and behind it, a stable. Next to that, the horse run where my aunt rode on weekends stretched toward the hillside. On the far right side of the yard there was a small guesthouse where the caretaker lived with his wife Rosa and his son Carlos. Between that and the main house, a large pen held loud mama and papa goats and two babies, called *kids*. The animals were Gwendolyn's, and she'd told me more than once to keep my hands off them. She said if I pet them they'd bite me, even though she pet them all the time.

The goat kids were super cute. Sheba was a little bigger than Shena, and Sheba was black and brown, where Shena was all black. Sometimes Gwendolyn would put the kids on leashes and parade them around the backyard, pretending they were show animals. Once I even overheard her talking to herself like she was announcing, "Sheba and Shena: Queen Goats of the Parade!" According to my cousin, she was also the only one allowed to feed them snacks, like dried fruit. Hello. If dried apricots made goats' gas smell as bad as mine did the one time I ate them, I'd stick to feeding my goats sugar cubes and grass.

Off to my left, the ocean roared and rumbled in the distance, and I could faintly smell it, fresh and cool. Past the end of the yard, the ragged Shadow Hills climbed toward the sky.

A curving row of pine trees grew near the back of the property. They were planted close together and stood straight and tall, as if they were guarding whatever was hiding behind them. I looked between two of the pines and spotted a row of steppingstones leading to a rusty metal gate. After slipping between the trees and hopping across the stones, I leaned forward and peeked through the gate. Then I just stared.

There was a strange and beautiful room on the other side.

The sun sank a little lower in the sky and the house-keeper, Rosa, stood behind the kitchen window and rang the dinner bell. If only I had more time to explore! My secret spot would have to wait.

4
Drumming in the Hills

Sunday night I looked out the window into the inky darkness with a smile on my face. Something awesome had already happened: I discovered a special hiding place on my very first day at my cousin's. Maybe this meant I would have good luck at my new school, too.

Then my stomach sank. *New school.* I would be walking down the halls of Malibu Middle first thing in the morning, where the only person I knew was Gwendolyn. Thinking about it made me really nervous. *Think positive, Skylar*, Grandpa would say. So I decided to try.

Maybe it wouldn't be so bad starting summer school in Malibu, right by the beach. There might be some cute boys in my class, and a cool girl that could become my new BFF. I pictured a tan girl with long blonde hair showing me around Malibu Middle School. Seconds later redheaded Alexa popped into mind and I felt instantly guilty. OK, not my new BFF. Just a *summer* BF. Or just a new F. Nobody could replace Alexa.

I pulled out my phone and texted her: Hope u have fun at camp. Miss u. Found an awesome spot in backyard. Wish u wr here to help me explore. N 2 go 2 school w me. XOXO S.

My phone chirped a minute later: Me 2. I cant text at camp. Agenst ruels unles mergncy. Mabey I can sneek. Wsh we cd both stay home. OXOX .A

My alarm would go off early in the morning, so I decided to get my stuff ready for school before I went to bed. First I picked up my Porta-detective kit. I'd chosen a metal carryall the size of a small lunchbox to contain my portable detective tools. It was pink with leopard spots and it locked with a small key. Hopefully anyone who saw it would think it was just my lunch, or a make-up kit or art supplies.

The rectangular container actually held a miniature version of my most important equipment: a penlight, small magnifying glass, rolled-up measuring tape, and a square of soft wax for taking impressions. There was also a smaller fingerprinting set called a Uniprinter, since it was just big enough to take one print. It contained a tiny vial of powder, a one-inch square stamp pad, and matching tablet of paper. Unzipping the plastic pouch inside my notebook, I checked to make sure I had everything I needed for class. Pen, pencil, eraser, gum eraser, ruler. Put my notebook and Porta-detective kit in my backpack and I was good to go.

Sort of. Thinking about going to Gwendolyn's school had me worried. I didn't know my way around Malibu Middle, and I didn't have a single friend there either. *How would I find my classroom? What if the Malibu locals were stuck-up and picked on me? Why couldn't I just stay home at my aunt's house and investigate the secret spot I'd found behind the gate in the backyard?*

I put some quarters in my change purse in case there was a snack machine, and double-checked my backpack to make sure I had everything I needed.

After I picked out a cute pair of shorts and a pink top, I set out one of my new bras. All of my bras were new since I hadn't been wearing them for very long. Unfortunately, they were also the smallest possible size. I painted my toenails pink to match my striped flip-flops and set my thongs down next to my outfit.

Feeling a little hyper like I couldn't sleep quite yet, I thumbed the combination on my detective kit locks and opened it. I pulled my pink Super-Zoom binoculars out of their pocket and knelt down in front of the window. My aunt's words echoed in my brain: *Stay out of the hills at night.*

Why?

I'd heard rumors that crazy people lived in tents up in Shadow Hills, and if you went up there after dark you could disappear forever. Climbing the hillside at night sounded about as fun as squeezing Gwendolyn's pimples, but whenever someone told me not to do something I wanted to know the reason. Suddenly I needed to find out if the rumors were true. I focused my binoculars and stared through them at the mountainside.

It was dark as an armpit and I couldn't see a thing.

As I looked into the blackness, a rhythmic drumming sounded from far away, like hands beating softly on congas. A slow steady tempo echoed out of the hillside. As I concentrated, trying to figure out what it was, the drumming faded away until I wasn't sure if I'd ever heard it at all. Was it just a car stereo, the bass pumping hard down the street—or something else?

One of the goats started to bleat. Its high-pitched call sounded like a silly giggle. Then the others chimed in, forming a whiny chorus. I closed my window and climbed into bed, wondering if I would get any sleep before my first day at a new school.

* * *

Monday morning after my shower I slipped my arms through skinny elastic straps, then fumbled around trying to fasten my new bra behind my back. I got ahold of both ends but couldn't get it hooked. Finally I spun the flimsy bra around and fastened it in front of my chest, then turned it back around and yanked the straps up over my shoulders. When I looked up, the mirror over the cupboards on the short side of the room caught my reflection. I looked nervous and like I needed a tan. I threw on my top, shorts, and flip-flops, and brushed my hair. I'd barely finished getting ready when Aunt Caroline warned that I had to hurry and eat breakfast or we'd miss the bus.

No time to text Alexa. I grabbed my backpack and headed for the kitchen. Gwendolyn was there ahead of me, shoveling in cereal. "Take your pick," my aunt said, setting three boxes of cereal and a small plate of sliced banana in front of me. "And put some banana on top. While you eat, we'll go over the house rules." She set a list down next to my bowl. *I knew it.* "Milk or juice?"

There was a carton of each in front of my empty glass. "Milk, thank you." I poured some, hoping it would settle my nervous stomach.

"Jim and I both work until five so you need to check in with one of us as soon as you get home from school each day. Call us from the house phone, not your cell, so I know you got home safely."

And so Caller ID will tell you where I am, I thought.

"The groundskeeper and his wife will be here until we get home from work. Rosa will make your lunch. Din-

26

nertime is six-thirty, and we eat as a family every night, no exceptions." I skimmed the rest of the list while she talked. They were the same rules I had at home. *Make your bed. Dirty clothes go in the hamper, not on the floor. Carry your plates to the sink. 8:00 curfew on weeknights, 10:00 on weekends. Need permission to go to someone else's house and a parent's phone numbers, home and cell. The beach, horses, and pool are off limits without an adult present. The hills are off limits, period.* I wasn't worried about breaking any house rules. What I was worried about was going to a new school where I didn't know my way around and didn't have any friends.

"I'll drive you to the bus stop today to show Skylar where it is. Hurry up girls, finish your breakfast. Gwendolyn can't afford to get a tardy. Can you, Gwendolyn?"

My cousin looked up at her, sulky. "*I'm* done," she said, showing my aunt her empty bowl. Like we knew whose fault it would be if we were late to school.

"Me too," I said. "Let's do this."

By the time my aunt dropped us off at the bus stop my hands were sweating. She had to pull into a parking lot so we could climb out without being hit by the cars flying past us on Pacific Coast Highway. The sky was pale blue, and the last of the morning fog was fading away to nothing. Exactly how I imagined myself at my new school.

"Be sure to show Skylar around the campus," my aunt told Gwendolyn, who barely nodded. I knew I'd be finding my way around all by myself. "And both of you check in when you get home."

We ran across the lot just as the bus pulled up to the stop. My cousin lumbered up the steps, heading for the back so she wouldn't have to sit near me. The bus stank worse than Gwendolyn's house. I looked at all the unfamiliar faces, heading for the first empty seat I saw.

A tall African-American boy sitting by the window tried to move over and make room for me, but his legs were so long they were touching the seat in front of us. His feet were huge. Long, thin arms held a sketchpad. I squished onto the seat next to him with one butt cheek hanging off the side of the bench, holding onto my backpack straps. As the bus rumbled down the coast, he opened his sketchpad and started to draw. I snuck a peek.

"Wow," I said, as he put the finishing touch on a fairy's wing. "That's so good."

He looked up and his dark eyes were wide, like people didn't compliment him very often. "Thanks. Ain't no thing," he said, erasing a tiny line on one feather that he apparently didn't like. He ran a hand over very short hair, frowning at his pad.

"No, I like to draw too, but that's excellent," I insisted. *Maybe he's in my art class*, I thought, but was too nervous to ask.

"You new?" He looked at me sideways. Like I amused him.

"Yeah." I fumbled with the buckle on my backpack. "I'm new."

"What's your name?" The bus hit a bump and we both lurched off the seat. Out came the eraser.

"Skylar. Skylar Robbins."

"Rudy Dean, new girl." He gave me a shy smile and

went back to drawing.

Outside the window a surfer bailed off a wave, falling backward into the water as his board shot up in the air. We turned a few corners, and before I was ready we pulled up to Malibu Middle School. Fortunately my parents went easy on me and agreed that I could just take an art class. They must have felt guilty about ditching me at Gwendolyn's or it would have been history and science. I got off the bus with a clog of kids pushing me forward.

I climbed down the steps and waited nervously for my cousin to come off the bus. "Where's room 31?" I hitched my heavy backpack higher onto my shoulder, wondering why I'd bothered to bring my Porta-detective kit. I didn't feel like investigating anything. All I wanted to do was go home.

Gwendolyn got a gleam in her eye and pointed across the campus to a far corner. "Over there. Behind the basketball courts." I stood on my tiptoes and tried to see past several long, L-shaped buildings. Way behind them there was a P.E. area where I saw some basketball hoops. I couldn't see anything beyond the courts. My cousin hurried off, leaving me to find my way on my own.

Rudy Dean turned around and looked at me. "She lies," he said. "Room 31 ain't behind no basketball court." It figured. "You in art?" I nodded. "Me too. Come on," he said, leading me the opposite way from where Gwendolyn had pointed.

All of the fog had burned off and the air started to get muggy. Typical Malibu summer: I felt like I was about to get sweaty even though it wasn't really hot out. Every open hallway looked the same: long and gray, lined with lockers on one side and packed with students. Rudy was a whole foot taller than almost everyone else and he walked fast. I almost had to trot to keep up with him and wiped my shiny forehead with the back of my hand.

We hurried into the classroom at the last second before the bell. All around the room, two-person desks were pushed together facing each other, making seating for four. Rudy gave me a quick nod, then sat down with three other boys. Too shy to sit with a gang of cute girls that were gossiping away like they'd been friends forever, I took a chair at a totally empty table. The bell rang.

"Good morning, class. I'm Miss Yamato," the teacher said. Her dark blue skirt and jacket were a little loose on her and looked brand new. Her hair was straight and black, and the ends were so blunt it looked like she'd just gotten a haircut yesterday. She was short and thin, with a small chest like mine. Miss Yamato wrote her name on the board and then the door opened and another student poked her head inside.

A mane of curly black hair framed her face. Her high cheekbones and pointed chin made a soft triangle. "Sorry I'm late," the girl announced, bouncing into the room. Spotting the empty seats at my table, she ran over and grabbed the chair next to mine. "Sorry," she said again, shrugging and smiling at the teacher. Then she looked at me and rolled her eyes. They were bright green and shaped like a cat's. "I'm Katrina," she told me. "But everyone calls me Kat."

"I'm Skylar." I wanted a cool name too, and had a sudden impulse. "My friends call me Sky."

"Awesome." Kat smiled and I felt excited, as if a brand

30

new part of my life had just begun. Her piercing green eyes also made me a little nervous. Like whatever happened next, good or bad, would be out of my control.

Miss Yamato took roll in a very soft voice so we all had to be quiet and pay attention. One of the boys at Rudy's table was hearing-impaired. He had short red hair and wore hearing aids in both ears. An interpreter in a blue smock stood near the teacher, signing everything she said. I found out later her name was Sue. When the teacher called, "Andy," Sue's eyes widened.

She must have signed his name, because the redheaded boy raised his hand and said, "Heah." I tried to pay attention to Miss Yamato but it was more fun to watch the interpreter.

"Our first project this summer will be making a stained-glass window. This exercise is going to teach you all how to see differently." The teacher passed out pencils and one sheet of drawing paper each, and I wondered how we could possibly make a stained-glass window out of a piece of paper and a pencil.

"I will hand out a list of the supplies you will need to buy for Wednesday. Bring your notebooks to write against. We're going for a walk." She led us outside and onto a large grassy area, and told us to sit down and look up at the sky. The sky was dotted with chunky white clouds shaped like puzzle pieces. "The clouds represent positive space. The shapes made by the blue sky in between them are known as negative space. Sketch the shapes you see in the negative space. Everyone understand?" Miss Yamato looked around to make sure everyone was nodding.

Feeling happy for the first time since my parents

dropped me at Gwendolyn's, I looked over at Andy. The interpreter had a questioning look on her face. Sue flicked her index finger up by her forehead with her palm facing back. I read her lips: "Understand?" She mouthed while she flicked, and the redheaded boy nodded.

"You will use them later for your stained-glass designs," Miss Yamato told us.

I wondered if Kat was watching the interpreter too, and glanced sideways. She wasn't paying attention to the teacher or to anyone else.

Kat had sketched a black crow in the margin of her notebook and was darkening its wings intensely. She caught me staring and nodded, like we were sharing an important secret.

5
A Note in Backward Writing

unt Caroline took me to an art supplies store after school on Tuesday. When we came back to class on Wednesday everyone brought tubes of "liquid lead" and hard sheets of clear plastic. After setting the plastic down on top of our sketches, we squirted out wavy lines of silver-colored goo, tracing our designs. Then we cleaned up the edges with Q-tips.

"When you are finished with the liquid lead you can take a break while it hardens," Miss Yamato said.

Rudy Dean held his glass up to the light and looked through it. From two tables over I could see he'd added a moon with an eerie face in between his cloud shapes. It wasn't part of the assignment but it looked really good. Andy pointed at it and signed something quickly to his interpreter, who smiled as she translated to Rudy.

I finished with my liquid lead, and while I waited for it to firm up I looked around the room. Missing Alexa, I fingered my cell. My dad always had to have the latest gadget, so when the new iPhones came out, he gave his old one to my mom and I got hers. The face was scratched and it was an older model, but it had a cool pink skin and it worked. Sneaking my phone out of its case, I glanced at the teacher. Using cells during class was forbidden in my old school and I didn't know what the rules were here. Maybe I could send Alexa a quick text from under my desk and no one would notice. She couldn't text me back, but whatever. I wanted her to know I was missing her.

When I scanned the classroom I noticed Kat writing strangely on a sheet of paper. At first I thought that she was left-handed, until I looked again. Kat's right hand was moving quickly across the page, writing from *right to left*. She caught me staring and gave me a quick smile. The way she caught my eye said the message was meant for me. I stuffed my cell back in my backpack. Kat folded up the note and passed it under our desk. I couldn't believe it.

Here is what it looked like:

The skater in the blue shirt sitting by the cupboards is SO cute!

At first I thought it was a secret code. Then I realized she had been writing backward.

"You can turn it over and hold it up to the light and read it through the back, or hold it up to a mirror—if you can't read it," Kat challenged. I concentrated and figured out what it said without turning it over. Then I looked across the room at the boy in the blue shirt. He *was* cute. He had blond, sun-streaked hair and a dark tan. There was a picture of a surfer on his T-shirt, and he'd stashed a skateboard under his seat.

I looked back at Kat's note. "How do you do that?"

"It's easy. You just learn how to make the letters backward. Kind of like drawing negative space." When Kat laughed, I noticed a lavender stone dangling from a chain around her neck.

"That's really pretty," I said pointing at her necklace. "What kind of stone is it?"

"It isn't a stone," Kat said. "It's an amulet."

"An amulet? What's—"

"It's for protection."

This sounded interesting. "Protection from who?"

Kat looked around to see if anyone was listening. No one was, but she lowered her voice anyway. "Not protection from *who*, protection from *what*."

"OK," I said impatiently, "from what?"

Kat rubbed the lavender stone. "Protection from *evil*."

Evil. *Really?* Did Kat think something evil could happen, right here at Malibu Middle? This kind of made me feel like looking over my shoulder, but I didn't.

Then I felt a little twinge, picturing my aunt twisting her fingers in the kitchen as she looked up into Shadow Hills. Maybe there was more to Malibu than guys surfing and movie stars' homes with walls of windows. I was dying to make a note on my pad about this and to ask Kat more questions, but Miss Yamato walked over to check on our projects so we had to stop talking.

When the liquid lead was dry, we filled in our negative spaces with blue glass stain. The unstained parts of the glass were shaped like clouds, and we filled them in with white crackle stain. I painted the stain in a swirling pattern, proud of how real my puffy clouds looked. Then I looked over at Kat's project. "What are you doing?" I asked, wondering if she would get in trouble.

"Making mine storm clouds." Kat squirted liquid lead inside her cloud shapes and smeared it around with a Q-tip. "There. That looks much better." She held up her stained-glass window. Her clouds looked dark and threatening and she fingered her amulet.

6
Invisible Ink

Before dinner I ran downstairs and found my aunt in the entryway, punching numbers into the security keypad. "Hi Skylar." She looked up at me. "I was just adding you to the security system. Your birthday is your code. Don't forget," she said, smiling. I heard a series of beeps before she turned around.

"Thanks, Aunt Caroline," I said. "I won't forget. Look what I made." I showed her my stained-glass window. Then I looked up through the second-story skylight into the sky. Noticing the shapes between the clouds first, I realized Miss Yamato really had taught us to see differently.

"That's beautiful," Aunt Caroline said, touching the edge of the plastic.

Just then Gwendolyn poked her face around the corner. "That looks breakable. Sure hope we don't have an earthquake." She laughed and scurried into the living room, holding a fan magazine in one hand and a big bag of Doritos in the other.

"Don't pay any attention to her," Aunt Caroline said. "She's not going to touch your property. *Are you*, Gwendolyn?" She didn't answer. "Consequences," my aunt called. It sounded weak, even to me. No one had ever been able to control my cousin.

I went upstairs and hid my artwork in my closet so an earthquake named Gwendolyn wouldn't wreck it. When I looked around the room, my eyes went right to the closet.

My hiding spot didn't feel the least bit safe. If she made any effort, my cousin would find it. Grandpa's advice came to mind: *Think ahead, Skylar. Collect evidence when you have the opportunity in case you need proof later.*

Thank you.

I snuck into my cousin's bathroom and swiped her drinking glass, picking it up carefully by pinching it at the bottom. Holding it by the base so I wouldn't smear her prints, I sped back through the halls. Rounding the corner by the picture of the clown in the plaid jacket, I bolted down the hall to the rose room. I unlocked my detective kit and pulled out the fingerprinting materials. After holding Gwendolyn's glass up to the light, I found a big greasy print right in the center. I dusted it with powder. Using a soft brush, I very gently wiped most of the powder away. A black fingerprint stuck to the glass. I covered it with a piece of clear tape, carefully pressed it down, and lifted the fingerprint.

"Got you."

I pasted the tape onto a Case Solution card and Gwendolyn's fingerprint was safely trapped. Using one of my secret marker pens, I wrote "Gwendolyn" on it in invisible ink.

Case Solution:

\# _____

Gwendolyn

Then I slipped the card into an evidence envelope, and wiped off my prints and the excess powder. After I put her glass back in its spot, I went into the closet and pulled out my creative writing notebook. Curling up on the alcove seat, I printed the alphabet backward. It was easier than I thought it would be. When I tried writing a backward sentence it looked just like Kat's note. Turning the paper over and holding it up to the mirror, I realized I had made some of my *a*'s forward, but that was my only mistake. I decided to write backward in my diary from now on in case Gwendolyn found it.

Creeping into my slanted closet, I took my diary out of the hatbox. Kneeling on the rose-patterned cushions in the alcove, I slowly printed a diary entry backward:

Dear Diary,

Fortunately my teacher is nice and art is fun so far. I already met a nice boy named Rudy Dean who's a really good artist, and I made a cool friend named Kat who showed me how to write backward-a new secret code! But those are the only good things because I really miss my mom and dad. This house smells and Gwendolyn is not being very nice to me-no surprise. I lifted her fingerprint in case she tries anything, and I know she will.

After that, I turned on my iPhone and Googled *sign language.*

The next morning I took the early bus to summer school so I'd have time to write a backward note before class.

The blond skater who sits by the cupboards is very cute. Why do you need protections? Love Sky

I folded up the paper into a tight square and set it on Kat's chair. The door opened and Andy came in. His interpreter wasn't there yet. I waited until he looked my way and spelled *hi*. It was easy. For *h*, I just pointed my first two fingers to the right with my palm facing forward. Then I made a fist while I raised my pinky to sign the *i*.

Andy's mouth fell open. He walked right up to me and started signing—way too fast for me to understand.

Oh no, I thought. His lips were moving but no words were coming out; just a few sounds that I couldn't understand. His fingers flew like he thought I knew sign language as well as I knew English. I'd made a big mistake, and I didn't know how to stop him. He looked so happy. And he just kept signing.

As my cheeks turned red I shook my head, raised my hand, and said, "Wait, I don't understand."

Andy must have read my lips because he slowed right down. He rubbed his fist in a circle with his fingers to his chest and mouthed, "Sorry." Then he drew one index finger across his other palm and said, "Wha." Andy pointed at me and said, "You." Then he stuck out the first two fingers of each hand, crossed and tapped them. "Nay?"

Now I was really embarrassed. I'd downloaded a fingerspelling chart the night before, but I hadn't practiced the letters hard enough. I couldn't even remember how to make a *K*. I didn't want to embarrass Andy by writing him a note, but I didn't know what else to do. So I said, "My name is Skylar," while looking him in the eye, and then wrote *Skylar* on a piece of paper and held it up. I'd already forgotten my cool nickname.

"You know wha, Sylah? I tee you how to sigh." Andy gave me a big smile and then sat down at his desk. He was going to teach me how to sign, and he looked like he couldn't wait. I promised myself I'd memorize the sign language alphabet, tonight.

Kat walked in behind a tall blonde girl with a big chest—one of the popular girls I was too shy to sit with on the first day. The blonde put her hand on the cute skater's arm and giggled. Kat looked at them and rolled her eyes at me. When she saw the note on her seat she smiled. She sat down and carefully unfolded it in her lap, reading it really fast without turning it over and holding it up to the light or anything. Tearing a piece of notebook paper out of her spiral, she dashed off a backward note to me. It took me a minute to figure out what it said:

We all need protection—from evil spirits and bad luck. Find an oval stone and we'll do the spell to turn it into an amulet. By the way, I'm a 5.

7
Forgotten Garden

After school Gwendolyn had piano lessons, so I finally had a chance to investigate the hidden place I'd stumbled across in the backyard. I checked in with Aunt Caroline and stashed a few items from my Porta-detective kit in the pockets of my jeans: a mini-magnifying glass, my penlight, and my phone, in case I wanted to take pictures. Running down the stairs and through the kitchen, I escaped into the yard unseen.

Casually walking outdoors, I ran by the stream and past the weeping willows. The groundskeeper was mowing the lawn, but he didn't even notice me. The stable and guesthouse were off to my right. To my left, so many different types of trees fought for space that the yard looked like a tangled forest. Thin sun lit up one side of the giant oak outside my window, but the crooked, shadowed branches on the other side looked like grasping arms. I hopped across the stream, hurried up to the jagged row of pines, took a deep breath, and passed between them.

As my feet hit each steppingstone, my fingertips brushed the ferns growing on either side of the walkway. Their cool green fronds were moist and soft. It felt like I was leaving my cousin's backyard behind and moving into somewhere special, private, and hidden. Just past the ninth stone there was a rusty metal gate, its pattern twisting and turning with curlicues. Fortunately, it wasn't locked. I unhooked the latch and the gate let out a warning creak as I pushed it open.

I took my first step inside a rectangular outdoor room. The gated garden had no ceiling, just four brick walls that opened to the sky. It was almost as big as my aunt's living room, and there was so much to see that I couldn't look around fast enough. I closed the gate behind me and started to explore.

A long time ago this had been someone's hidden garden. I turned around slowly, pulling out my cell and taking pictures. Every corner was wild and beautiful. The ground was overgrown with weeds and orange poppies. Brightly flowering vines grew up and over the brick walls in a giant tangle, but some of the branches were dead and black. On the left side, a few feet before the garden ended, there was a small fountain made of crumbling clay, the same color as my untanned skin. The old clay bowl was just a little bigger than my bathroom sink, and looked like it hadn't had water in it for a very long time. A rusted water pump lay in the center of the bowl, crusted with dirt and dead leaves. Its wires were split and rotten, so I knew the fountain wouldn't work. An old-fashioned iron stool sat in front of it, caked with rust. Its faded pink cushion was stained and damp.

In the far right corner of the garden there was an empty fishpond the size of a small hot tub. Surrounding the pond, what was once a circle of thick bushes had become a dry skeleton. Knobby bones held each other's wrists like they were afraid to fall in. Tall weeds wrapped around the dead branches and sprouted tiny lavender flowers. Vivid green moss covered the bottom of the pond, and white-flowering weeds poked through cracks in the plaster. I leaned over to sniff them but they didn't smell good. I wanted to know more about this garden immediately. Aiming my phone, I spun around slowly, taking a video to send to Alexa and to examine later.

Big patches of nasturtiums decorated the left corner of the garden. Their flowers were nothing like the plain red, yellow, or orange ones I had seen before. I bent down and parted round leaves that looked like green lily pads. Pale yellow flowers with bright magenta stripes grew next to pumpkin-colored blossoms with rich brown splashes in the center of each petal. Bright red mouths screamed in the center of tangerine-colored nasturtiums. I wanted to pick a bouquet, but I knew these magically colored flowers could give away my hiding spot, so I left them alone.

The sunlight was fading, and a chilly white fog edged forward like a slow-moving blanket. I stepped back through the weeds, watching the ground so I wouldn't crush anything that was still alive. A black crow flapped its wings hard and soared over my head toward the house, squawking loudly.

Before walking out of the garden I turned around for one last look. Pointing my cell, I took a few more pictures to share with Alexa. Then I remembered that she couldn't text and put my phone away, missing my friend. When I got to the gate I happened to glance down and my mouth fell open. Resting by my right foot was a perfectly oval stone.

8
A Small Dark Window

The stone was pearl gray and pink with dark speckles. Thin lavender veins circled around to the other side. It was unusually shiny for something that had been resting in the dirt. "This will become my amulet," I thought, popping it into my pocket.

Zipping up my sweatshirt, I walked through the gate and hurried across the lawn, wrapping my arms around my body. The cold, damp air blowing through the trees whipped my hair into my face. I looked up at the top floor of the house, wondering if I could pick out my room. Recognizing the twisted oak tree, I looked through it and spotted the bay window in the rose room. A little higher up, a small dark window reflected crooked black branches, and behind them, Shadow Hills.

Goose bumps rose on my arms as I remembered Aunt Caroline's warning when we passed the hidden staircase: Stay out of the attic. The attic loomed behind that window, dark and eerie. It was right over my bedroom. I hoped I wouldn't have nightmares about my dead great-aunt's ashes blowing around above my head.

When I got back to the rose room I practiced the sign language alphabet over and over. Then I took out my backpack and zipped my oval stone into the inside pocket. I couldn't wait to show Kat and find out how to turn it into an amulet. I also wondered what "I'm a 5" meant.

* * *

The next day in art class I found out. Kat was already there and I found a note on my seat. This one wasn't backward. It was a chart and a set of instructions that looked like this:

```
1  2  3  4  5  6  7  8  9
A  B  C  D  E  F  G  H  I
J  K  L  M  N  O  P  Q  R
S  T  U  V  W  X  Y  Z
```

Add up the numbers that match the letters in your first name. Then add the two numbers in the total together until you reach a single digit. This is your number. This is what it means:

1 ambitious, powerful, red
2 introvert, emotional, silver
3 humorous, loyal, yellow
4 intuitive, spiritual, lavender
5 friendly, extrovert, orange
6 pleasant, accommodating, pink
7 psychic, healing, blue
8 materialistic, successful, green
9 jealous, impulsive, purple

This was absolutely cool—I love secret codes and charts. I did the math in my head. If I used *Skylar*, I was a *5* too. If I used *Sky*, I was a *1*. *Ambitious and powerful* had my name all over it, so I decided to call myself *Sky* from now on. I had just started figuring out Gwendolyn's number when the teacher started to talk.

For this week's project we had to pick a partner. Andy was walking toward me, so I waved and smiled.

Kat noticed. "Want to be partners?" she asked really fast.

Andy was almost right in front of me when I said, "Sure. OK." He took one look at Kat's face and stopped smiling.

Andy signed as he spoke. "You alreh ha a patnah?" he asked me, pointing at Kat. *You already have a partner?*

"Yes," I said, nodding. I rubbed my fist in a circle on my chest like he'd shown me before. *Sorry.* I felt bad, but I really did want a girl for a partner.

"It OK. Thi how you sigh *yes*," Andy said. He bounced his fist in the air twice. I copied him and he nodded. "Goo job, Sylah. Neck tie I tea you how to sigh *no*." Andy smiled and looked around for someone else to team up with.

Kat looked at his back. "What was that?" she laughed. "Like you would ever be his partner." She shook her head.

"Maybe I would," I said. "I don't care that he's hearing-impaired." I looked at my new friend, not quite sure what she meant.

"It's not that," she said, staring at me. "He's a *ginger*."

Wait a minute. *Are you kidding me?*

"So what if he's got red hair?" I didn't get this at all. Some of the girls at home made fun of Alexa for the same reason. It was the dumbest thing I'd ever heard.

Kat opened her purse and peered in as if the conversation was over. Apparently whatever was at the bottom of her purse was much more interesting than my opinion. Then Kat gave me a serious look that turned into a smile. "You're right. Want some?" she asked, offering me her lip gloss.

I didn't want to lose the only real friend I'd made so far. So I smiled while I shook my head. "No thanks."

"Good morning, class," Miss Yamato said softly as she passed out a sheet of instructions. "The purpose of your next project is to teach you to work creatively with others to achieve a goal. Your assignment is to design a special container and explain why it is perfect for its contents." Kat looked at me and grinned. She scribbled a quick backward note.

This is a great project!

I reached inside my art supplies bag and pulled out the oval stone I found in the forgotten garden. "Kat, look." Uncurling my fingers, I showed her the pink and gray rock sitting on my palm. I hoped she would remember telling me to find an oval stone and promising to help me turn it into an amulet. Kat took it from me and looked at both sides.

"This is *perfect* for your amulet." She handed it back and my heart thumped, wondering what we could do to make my stone powerful.

We got to spend the next ten minutes talking to our partners, trying to come up with creative ideas about our containers. I looked over at Andy's table. He'd partnered up with Rudy, who was talking excitedly and gesturing. The interpreter's fingers were flying. I wished I knew sign language—it looked so cool.

I also wished I had an idea for the project, but my mind was blank. At first, all I could think of were the old hatboxes in the slanted closet that hid my diary, and the locked case protecting the items in my detective kit. I looked around the room, trying to come up with something. A wall of white cupboards towered to my left and the chalkboard faced me. Miss Yamato sat at her desk, reading a textbook. The only windows were behind me. Across the room, the cute skater was trying to flirt with the girl with the big chest. She ignored him, texting someone with her cell hidden under her desk. Rudy Dean made a quick sketch in his pad and showed it to Andy, who smiled and nodded.

"I don't have any ideas yet," I admitted to Kat. "How about you?"

"I have a bunch of them," she said, leaning toward me. "We can decorate a special box for our amulets. We can go down to the beach and collect stones with different powers and weave a basket for them. We can embroider spirit pouches and fill them with herbs, feathers, incense, and seashells. We can use our leftover liquid lead and glass stain and decorate a candle holder with Wiccan symbols."

My new friend was amazing. "What's Wiccan?" I mouthed.

She looked around. No one was listening.

"Witchcraft." She waited to see how I'd react, then continued. "I'll sleep over Saturday night and introduce you."

"OK. I'll ask. Introduce me to what?"

Kat looked at me. "Everything Wiccan. I know all about it. And I'll let you in."

A nervous tingle shot down my spine. My brain was spinning. I decided to put my plan to escape from Malibu on hold for now.

9
Extra Shadows

Aunt Caroline agreed to let Kat sleep over Saturday night so we could work on our art project. Her sister dropped her off after lunch with her sleeping bag and backpack. Kat looked around my aunt's house as we walked through the living room toward the stairs. "This house is powerful," she whispered. "That spiral staircase is wicked cool."

We took her things up to my slanted room and I unlocked my detective kit. "What's that?" Kat peered inside and looked at all of my goodies.

"My detective kit," I said proudly. Kat stared at me with her mouth forming a small *o*. "It has every tool I need to solve a crime. For example," I pulled the magnifying glass out of a pocket and held it up, "my magnifying glass and a flashlight."

"I feel something outside waiting for us to discover it. Let's go see what it is." Kat led the way down the stairs, and I looked over my shoulder to make sure Gwendolyn wasn't following us. We ran out the back door and hurried up the path. The sweet scent of hay and a faint smell of animal poop crossed on the breeze as we hopped over the stream.

A goat bleated from the other side of the yard and Kat looked at me. "Was that a goat?"

I nodded, and watched her face go still. "My cousin's. The little ones are cute, but they're loud. And stinky," I said, but Kat didn't answer. She looked past the pines and up into the mountains. The same place where Aunt Caroline always stared at dusk, worrying her fingers. "Why do they call those Shadow Hills?" I asked. A cloud slid past the sun, dimming the yard.

Kat didn't answer right away. She just stared mutely into the hillside, her eyes glassy. Finally, she turned to look at me. "Because there are more shadows than there should be, with the angles and the sunlight."

"What do you mean? There's like, extra shadows?" I asked, and Kat nodded seriously. "How can that—"

"The extra shadows were made on purpose."

"Made—what?"

Kat glanced back into the hills with a strange glint in her eyes. Like she knew something she wouldn't tell me. "You ever explore up there during a full moon?" She raised her eyebrows and looked at me sideways. It felt like a challenge.

"No. My aunt said I'm not allowed into the hills, especially after it gets dark." Staring up at the mountainside, I wondered if it was the setting sun that shifted the shadows, or something more sinister. "Why? What happens up there at night?"

Kat shook her head and walked a little faster. I could tell she was debating something. Weighing whether she should tell me some secret. The foggy air felt damp, and I wrapped my arms tightly around myself, like I was keeping something in. Or trying to keep something out.

Kat stopped suddenly and turned toward me. "OK, don't freak out."

The way she said it gave me the chills. Spine chills, not like my skin was cold from the ocean breeze. "Why?

What's wrong?" I asked, rubbing my arms. Like that would help.

She looked at me intensely. "You can't tell anyone."

I held out my pinky to swear, but Kat barely looked at it before she started walking again, even faster. She pointed into Shadow Hills and looked at me over her shoulder. "There's a coven called Demonia that practices up in the mountainside."

"What's a coven?" Maybe something I read about in *Twilight*? I grabbed her arm and made her stop walking.

She stared at me, like I really was a little dense. "Thirteen witches."

"What do they do up there?" I had a feeling I knew the answer, but needed Kat to confirm it.

"Black magic, Sky." She looked hard into my eyes. "My sister Diana told me all about Demonia, and they're evil."

"What do you mean?" My mouth went dry.

Kat's voice got dark and husky. "Like to replace wine in their ceremonies, they use water from a well where an unbaptized child drowned."

The breeze suddenly stopped, like it was waiting for my reply. I wondered if there were any wells nearby, and how often children fell into them. "And they—drink it?" I tried to swallow but my throat wouldn't move.

"Yes. They drink the well water. And the goat is the symbol of their leader. So keeping goats outside around here is a little dangerous, don't you think?" Kat started walking again and I had to hurry to keep up. It felt like she was leading me, instead of the other way around.

This was getting really creepy so I tried to make a

joke. "Not unless you stand behind them after they've eaten dried apricots." I waved my hand in front of my nose like I smelled goat farts, but Kat wasn't even close to smiling.

"I mean keeping them out in the open like that, where anyone could, you know, take one." She looked back at the goats and then at me.

"Take one? Steal a goat? Why would—"

But Kat just put one hand in the air and shook her head, like she shouldn't have to explain.

When we passed the weeping willows, Kat stopped walking and tilted her head as if she was listening. Then she smiled, like the conversation about drowning babies and stolen goats had never happened. "The vibrations here are awesome," she said quietly, bending down and looking at the earth. "We could find amethyst and even jade here if we're lucky. Those stones would be perfect for our baskets."

Kneeling down, I ran my fingers over the earth, looking through my magnifying glass for precious stones. I didn't find any, but I wasn't that surprised. I knew a better place for us to search.

"Follow me." I led her through the pine trees and down the fern-lined path, looking forward to sharing my secret place with my new friend. "I have something to show you."

"The vibrations are getting stronger," Kat said. We walked through the rusty gate and into the forgotten garden. "Oh Sky," she said in a hushed voice. "There is so much magic here." She looked around slowly like she was memorizing every detail. "This garden can be our sacred place: the doorway to another dimension."

Kat was the most exciting friend I'd ever had. Time to quit worrying about some coven practicing black magic in the hills behind Gwendolyn's yard. I couldn't wait to hear more about the doorway. "What do you mean?"

She stopped exploring and looked at me. "To perform spells, you need a private, sacred place where the vibrations are right. This garden is perfect. If you want to do magic—*white* magic," she looked like she was waiting for me to agree so I nodded quickly, "then we need to set up an altar, right here."

"OK," I agreed. "How do we do that?"

"First we need to find objects representing the four elements: air, fire, water, and earth." Kat pointed at the chipped fountain, perched unevenly on its cement base. "The chalice, or Spirit Bowl, represents water. In ancient times they just used a big seashell. This old fountain will make the perfect chalice. Does it work?"

I shook my head. "I doubt it."

"Doesn't matter. Then we need two candles, a wand for air, an athame—or sword—for fire, and a pentacle for earth."

I whipped open my notepad and started scribbling a list.

"An incense burner would be good too, but it's not mandatory," she added.

"Wait—what's a pentacle?"

Kat looked like she was surprised I didn't know. "It used to be a smooth, oval rock, marked with a five-pointed star. Now it can be anything that shows a star inside a circle."

Wondering where we could possibly find a sword, or if maybe we could make one, I felt really happy for the first time since my parents left. Even more excited than when I'd found the forgotten garden. I sketched a star inside a circle and wrote, "pentacle" underneath it.

"Why does a sword represent fire?" I asked. "Can't we just use a candle?"

"No. And it's *athame*, not sword."

"Spell it."

Kat quickly spelled *athame* while she walked farther into the garden. She pointed at some sweet-smelling green shrubs with little white flowers growing along the stems. "Look."

"What's that?"

"Jasmine. It gives psychic protection. If you wrap some around your amulet it will make it even stronger. Pick a little bit of it," she said. "We'll turn your oval stone into an amulet later. And here," she bent down by the pond and pointed to some silver-green leaves. "This is sage. It cleanses evil. Break off a sprig. If you burn some and wave it around it gives great protection."

"How do you know all this Harry Potter stuff?"

"Harry *Potter*? Puh-lease." She gave me a dirty look.

"Sorry." I knelt down and tore three sage leaves off their stems. "But how do you know all these spells and things?"

"From my sister Diana." Kat looked at me seriously. Like she was wondering if she could trust me with an important secret. "She's a witch." Kat stared into my eyes, waiting for my reaction.

I felt like I had to pass some test, and stayed quiet so

I wouldn't fail.

"And so am I," Kat said.

Wait a minute. *What?* I couldn't decide if this was the coolest thing I'd ever heard, or if it was kind of scary/creepy. "How can you be—I mean aren't you like thirteen years old?"

Kat laughed. "There's no age limit. Witchcraft isn't like driving. You don't like, 'take a test and get a license,'" she said, curling her fingers and making quotation marks in the air. Kat looked at me like I was a child who didn't make it to the bathroom on time. Then her whole face changed and she smiled nicely. "My sister's training me. She's been practicing for years. Diana's named after the Wiccan moon goddess."

"Goddess?" I repeated dumbly.

Kat spoke slowly in case I had trouble understanding new things. "The Goddess Diana was the queen of all witches, who she calls her Hidden Children. Diana ruled the night and gave light to the darkness. The moon is her sacred symbol."

"Oh." I had no idea what she was talking about and really felt like that slow child. "So your sister is a good witch?"

Kat laughed. "Yes. She's part of a coven called Wister. They practice white magic. I'm going to join too, as soon as I turn eighteen."

"But wait—I thought you said there's no age limit."

"To be a *witch*," Kat explained. "You have to be eighteen to join a coven. Usually covens are twelve women and one man, but Diana's coven is all females. They meet to pool their energy. It makes their spells more powerful."

I put the sage leaves in my pocket with the jasmine. "Are you serious?" Looking at Kat's green eyes and black hair that swirled like storm clouds, I thought that just maybe she was telling the truth.

"Of course. Diana has a magic herb garden. Next time I come over I can bring some cuttings, and we can plant what we need."

"OK," I agreed quickly, before she could change her mind. "What we need for what?"

"For our sachets. And for other things," she hinted, picking up a foot-long twig. "We can use this for the wand. Now let's try to find some good stones." We hunted for them on our hands and knees. Crawling through the garden slowly, we picked up trailing vines and piles of dead leaves and peeked underneath them. I aimed my flashlight through a leafless bush and into a corner. Behind the brittle branches, a shiny object glistened. I looked at it through my magnifying glass. A cool breeze lifted the hair off my neck as I turned to smile at Kat. "I found one." The stone was similar to my amulet, but this rock was round and larger with more purple veins.

"Excellent," she said, then went back to looking at the ground around the edge of the old fishpond. It wasn't long before Kat was grunting and pulling at something. "Amethyst," she said, holding up a dirty purple rock. "I *knew* it."

"How did you know?" Was she psychic? Maybe she was really a *seven*. I wondered if she would be if she factored in her last name.

"Shadow Hills are full of amethyst," she said, turning around to look up at them. Her forehead wrinkled before she looked back at me. "Keep digging. You'll find some. Then we have to do a ritual to cleanse the stones to make them powerful."

I could smell the moist earth as I dug into it. A minute later my fingers hit a hard object. I wiggled it back and forth and pulled out a sparkling stone. "Is this anything?" I showed it to her.

"That's quartz. Awesome. I knew we'd find great stones here." We scouted around until we each had three. Then we passed between the pines and carried them to the stream for the cleansing ritual.

"You have to either wash magic stones in salt water, or hold them under natural running water to remove any negative vibrations," she explained. We let the stream wash the dust and dirt off our rocks. When we picked them back up the amethyst and quartz sparkled like crazy. Even my little speckled rock looked happy. Before we went inside my aunt's house we took a last look inside the forgotten garden. "Whoever planted this garden really knew what she was doing," Kat said.

"What do you mean?" I asked, thinking of my great-aunt who had passed two years ago. Her almost-dead garden made me kind of sad. No one had sat on that moldy pink cushion in a long time.

"There are way too many magical elements to be here by chance. If we practice, I think we'll really be able to perform strong spells here," Kat said.

We walked across the steppingstones, and I looked up at the attic window above my bedroom. I touched Kat's shoulder and pointed. She stared up at the window and drew a large star in the air with her ring finger.

There was a shadow moving around behind the glass.

10
Oval Stone Amulet

During dinner Gwendolyn didn't say one word to Kat. It was like she was pretending I didn't have a friend over. Gwendolyn just chewed—occasionally with her mouth open—belched once or twice, and slurped her milk. Kat nudged me when Gwendolyn wasn't looking and rolled her eyes.

When the meal finally ended, Kat and I excused ourselves and went up to my bedroom. "This is the coolest room. That window's sick." As the last of the daylight disappeared and the shadows darkened, the trees outside my window started to look threatening. The oak's twisted branches stretched down into the dark backyard like arms with grasping hands. Fog filled the valley between the hills. It looked like something you could drown in.

We sat down on the cushioned bench and emptied our pockets. "We'll make a basket another time to hold the magic stones," Kat said. "Tonight we have to make your amulet. You need protection right away."

I fingered the rocks I'd rinsed in the stream. "From what?" The look on Kat's face made me nervous. *Whatever was roaming around the attic? Or whatever was happening up in Shadow Hills?*

"There are evil forces at work in this house." She pushed masses of black curls over her shoulders and stared at me with her piercing emerald eyes.

I looked up at the ceiling, wondering if she meant my dead great-aunt. "What do you mean?"

"Your cousin Gwendolyn. No offense, but she may be an evil spirit."

So it wasn't just me. "I think you're right."

"We'll take care of her later," Kat promised. "Don't worry, we won't do anything to her personally. We'll just weaken her powers. But first, your amulet. Can you go get some salt and a bowl of water? We'll also need a candle. You don't have a purple one, do you?"

"I don't think so. I know where there are red and green ones though, in the Christmas stuff."

"Get a red one, and we'll need to anoint it with oil."

"What's *anoint*?" I felt my forehead scrunched up.

Kat looked at me like, *Duh*. "Rub."

"OK. What kind?"

"Olive oil's fine and your aunt probably has some in the kitchen. Do you have any clear plastic and liquid lead left from making the stained-glass windows?" I pulled them out from the drawer where I kept my art supplies and held them up. "Good. Go get the candle and the olive oil, a bowl of water and some salt, and I'll make an altar."

Jogging down the stairs with my heart racing, I ran into the kitchen and stopped suddenly. My aunt was washing dishes and Gwendolyn was drying them. The saltshaker sat innocently on the kitchen table. When no one was looking, I shook some salt into my pocket and kept on walking. I knew the Christmas decorations were in the den closet, reached in and grabbed a red candle. Then I walked casually back into the kitchen. "Do you need any help?" I asked politely.

"Sure do." Gwendolyn tossed the towel at me and ran out of the room.

This was fine with me. They had almost finished the dishes, and now I had one less pair of eyes to worry about.

"Is it OK if we light a candle in my room?" I asked.

"Sure. Just be careful with the wax." Aunt Caroline kept looking at me while we dried the last things, like there was something she didn't know quite how to say. Or something she guessed I wouldn't want to hear. Finally she shook her head the slightest bit and said goodnight. My aunt started to walk away and a minute later I wished she'd just kept going. I could tell by the slow way she turned back to look at me that I wasn't going to like what she was about to ask me.

"My trainer will be here Saturday afternoon. How would you like to take a horseback riding lesson?" she asked, and my stomach plunged. "I can arrange it." Aunt Caroline smiled nicely at me, then cocked her head to one side when she saw the look on my face. "Is everything all right?"

I nodded. "Uh—it's very nice of you, but I'd rather not." I stared at my aunt's feet, embarrassed.

"Skylar?" She put her hands on my shoulders and I stiffened, forced to look up at her. To my horror, my eyes filled with tears.

"Yes." It came out in a whisper.

"Honey, do horses scare you?"

Oh God, she knows.

I shook my head. "Not really," I lied. "Well maybe a little." My aunt stared at me until I had to look away. "Please don't tell Gwendolyn," I mumbled.

"Your secret is safe with me," she said. "But a lesson with a professional might help you conquer your fear.

You don't have to decide now. Just think about it." The soft voice she was using made me realize that she'd known I was afraid of horses all along.

"I will," I promised. But I knew that what I'd be thinking about was ways to get out of it.

"OK," Aunt Caroline finally agreed. "Have fun with your friend, Sweetheart," my aunt said, planting a firm kiss on my cheek. This made me remember how much I missed my mom, and my throat started to ache. I had to open my eyes really wide to keep the tears back.

Where were my mom and dad right now? France? England? What time was it over there anyway? My dad told me there was an eight-hour time difference, but I didn't know if he meant earlier or later. Were they sound asleep, or sharing a buttery croissant at a sidewalk café in Paris? Maybe my parents were taking a mid-afternoon stroll down a cobblestone street in Spain. Or sipping thick coffee drinks after a gourmet dinner in Italy.

Did my mom and dad miss me? Were they even thinking about me at all? Once again I wished I were an undercover detective, and imagined how cool my life would be once I became one:

The U.S. government sent me to Italy on a Top Secret mission. As the Lear jet sped over the United States, I ducked into the First Class bathroom and put on my disguise. After pasting a thick brown moustache above my upper lip, I stretched a bald-spot wig over my head. I hid a listening device in my underwear and ran the wire up the back of my suit jacket. As soon as the airplane hit the ground I was off and running. Through the terminal, out the door, and into the cab line.

Jumping into a taxi and riding it to a bus stop, I took a bus two miles in the wrong direction to make sure I wasn't being followed. When I was sure no one was tailing me, I caught the Metro and rode it back to my parents' hotel. I had to be sure they were safe. Climbing up a fire escape on the side of the building, I looked through my night vision goggles until I spotted them. There they were.

As my parents sipped coffee at the outdoor café, I plugged in my earpiece. I adjusted the volume on my listening device in time to hear my mom say, "I sure do miss Skylar." Aiming a red laser beam into my dad's coffee cup, I spelled out a message I hoped he would read before he brought the cup up to his lips: "GO HOME NOW." Just then a bullet whizzed by my head. I climbed down the fire escape stairs and ran for my life.

Looking at the familiar counter in my aunt's kitchen, I tried to forget about what my parents were doing in Europe. Kat was waiting for me in my bedroom, and that made me feel less lonely. "Good night, Aunt Caroline. Thanks for letting Kat sleep over." She touched my shoulder and gave me a warm smile, then turned and walked out of the kitchen.

Quickly finding the olive oil and grabbing a salad bowl, I swiped a book of matches out of the cupboard where my uncle kept the barbeque stuff. Then I hurried up the stairs to the bathroom. I ran some water into the bowl and hurried back to the rose room. "Whew!" I breathed, closing the door.

I couldn't believe the sight in front of me. Kat sat cross-legged on the floor in the middle of a circle she'd made out of scarves and belts she found in the closet.

Magical piles rested at five equal points around the circle. Our speckled stones made up one point. Sage leaves sat at another. Amethyst was at the third, jasmine branches at the fourth, and quartz at the fifth. Kat leaned forward and drew lines with liquid lead on a leftover piece of clear plastic.

"What's that?" I asked.

"Our pentacle." She squirted out the last line. It looked like a regular five-point star inside a circle. Kat looked like she was about to let me in on something big. "The pentacle is used in protection, to symbolize the four elements and the spirit. We have to keep the star pointing away from us, so it is a symbol of Wicca. If it points toward us, it represents evil." Tucking my hair behind my ears, I sat down inside the circle next to Kat so we could both look at the pentacle with the star pointing away.

Gusty wind blew through the hills, rattling my window. The dark glass shuddered against the cold air pushing at it from outside. From far in the distance I heard a high-pitched wailing noise, like a woman weeping or an animal crying. It gave me goose bumps. "Did you hear that?" I asked Kat.

She glanced toward the alcove window, and then looked down at the pentacle. "Probably just the wind." Then her eyes slid up to meet mine, like she wondered if I believed her.

The oak tree's branches bowed and bent, scraping the wall below my bedroom and snapping against the small window in the attic above. It felt cozy to be inside. "I hope we don't need a lot of salt." Pinching along the bottom of my pocket, I brought up a few grains at a time, along with a little lint. I dropped them into the bowl of water. "Here's the candle and the olive oil."

"We have to rub the oil into the candle from the middle out to the ends. But first, we have to carve the candle's purpose down the side in our own magic alphabet."

"Backward writing?" I guessed.

"Exactly. Do you have something we can use to carve into the wax?"

I found an old barrette and pulled it open wide. "What do we write?"

Her eyes flicked toward the window again, so fast I almost didn't catch it. "Protect us from evil."

11
Protect Us From Evil

We took turns carving crude backward letters into the wax. "Next, we need to anoint the candle with oil and concentrate on our purpose as we rub it in," Kat said. We poured olive oil onto our fingertips and rubbed it into the candle from the middle to the ends. "Now we have to repeat, *Protect us from evil*, nine times," Kat said, and we did.

She lit the red candle and held it sideways over the pentacle until the drops of hot wax formed a small puddle. After standing the lit candle in the melted wax, she braced it with her fingers until the wax hardened. It stood straight up in the center of the liquid-lead star. "It is time for us to turn an ordinary stone into your amulet. Hand me my backpack."

I tossed it to her, then turned off my light and sat back down next to Kat inside the circle. Her eyes looked eerie in the glow of the flickering flame. She reached into a backpack pocket and pulled out a Baggie full of little white shells. Setting the biggest one in the bottom of the bowl of water, she made a crescent underneath it with nine others in the shape of a smile. Or a sliver of moon. Or horns.

"Next we charge the water to make it magical. Put your fingers together like this, so your index fingers and your thumbs form a triangle." She held her hands out, palms down, with her index fingers and thumbs touching each other. After I copied her she said, "Now inhale deep-

67

ly and picture the moon over our heads."

Just then a fierce gust of wind shook the house, making me flinch, as if nature had heard her call and was answering. Kat leaned over and blew three times through the triangle between her fingers. "Exhale three times onto the liquid in the chalice," she told me, "and visualize moonlight pouring down through your head, out with your breath, and onto the water, charming it."

When I'd finished breathing into the water I felt a little weak. Like a spirit had flown through me, leaving emptiness behind.

"Now we enchant the water," she said.

"I thought we just did that."

Kat looked at me, annoyed. "No, we just *charmed* it. Now we enchant it. Take your right hand, palm down and pass it over the water clockwise, nine times." I rotated my hand over the chalice and Kat held hers over mine, following my slow circles. "Now while I recite the spell, you blow on the water to disturb its surface."

This felt like rubbing my tummy and patting my head at the same time, but I managed to make circles with my hand while I blew on the water. "Now do the same thing with your other hand." We repeated the ritual, and then she dropped my oval stone into the water, mumbling a spell in what sounded like Latin. Of course I had never heard Latin before so I couldn't tell if she was just making up the words, but it was more fun to think it was real. "Imagine your amulet being filled with the protective power of Wicca." We stared at the stone in the bottom of the chalice as the red candle continued to burn.

"When you blow out the candle, as the smoke rises

from the wick and mingles with the air, so shall our spell become one with reality, and your amulet will become filled with the power to protect you. Concentrate on protection from evil as the smoke and air combine. You need it badly." She stared into my eyes. "Ready?" Just as I bent forward, we heard a sharp rap on my bedroom door.

"Oh no." I looked at Kat and held my breath.

"Kill the candle," she said. "Hurry!"

I blew out the candle, hoping desperately for protection from evil as my door handle jiggled and shook.

12
Angry Spirit

"Coming." I licked my fingers, pinched the wick, and tossed the dead candle into the closet. Then I stood up and waved my hands around, trying to get rid of the smoke. Kat tore the spread off my bed and tossed it across the magic circle, covering the chalice and our herbs and stones. I opened the door and looked down the dark, empty hall.

No one was there.

"It must have been Gwendolyn," I said, closing my door and turning on the light.

Kat smiled. "The door wasn't locked, was it?"

I shook my head.

"And she couldn't get in."

"But how—" I whipped my head sideways and stared at my door.

"The magic is working already."

This made the hair stand up on my arms. "You just gave me the chills."

"That wasn't me." Kat stared at me, letting her comment sink in. "Now we have to release the charge into running water." Holding the chalice carefully, she led me down the hall and found the bathroom.

I turned on the faucet and Kat handed me the chalice. "Now slowly empty the amulet water into the running water so they mingle as I recite the spell. Ready?"

I nodded, tipping the bowl.

"Water to water, the charge is well; stream meets

stream, complete the amulet's spell."

After the last of the water trickled down the drain, I followed her back to my bedroom. "Your amulet is very strong. It's time to make it into a necklace, and I think you should wear it all the time." Hunting around in my jewelry box, I took out a silver chain and held it up with a questioning look on my face. "That's perfect," she said. "Now you need a pocket to hold the amulet."

I pawed through my backpack, fishing out a leather change purse with a drawstring top. Opening it wide, I spilled out a few coins, and then showed it to Kat. "How about this?"

"The magic worked again. Slip your sacred stone inside. Add some sage for protection from evil, and a sprig of jasmine for spiritual defense. Then put it on."

After I put my necklace together, we cut a sword out of cardboard and covered it with tin foil. Then we drizzled glue onto the edges and sprinkled on colored glitter. I let the extra glitter fall into my trashcan and then set the sword on the dresser to dry.

Kat got into her sleeping bag. I turned out the lights and climbed into bed, wearing the amulet around my neck. Kat had hers on too.

I didn't realize then how badly we would need the protection.

I woke up suddenly in the middle of the night. I knew I had heard a strange noise, but foggy with sleep, I couldn't figure out what it was. Then I heard it again. A soft, batting sound, right over our heads.

"Kat. Wake up," I whispered.

"I'm awake. You heard it too?" Kat rustled around in her sleeping bag and sat up.

"Yes. It sounds like boxes are moving around up in the attic."

"They can't move around by themselves," Kat said. "Actually maybe they can, if the vibrations in this house are as strong as I think they are."

"Shh. Let's see if it happens again."

"We better hope it doesn't. Can you light the red candle? I think it will help."

I crept out of bed and lit a match. The burst of flame was like a firework in my dark room. She picked up the wand and handed me the tin foil-covered sword. The sparkling glitter glinted in the candlelight. "We need to make the sign of the pentacle at every entrance into the room to keep out anything evil."

I wished we had a stronger weapon. Something I knew I could really believe in. We drew large stars in the air in front of both windows and the doorway. I couldn't imagine how that could do any good, but we were both pretty creeped out so I figured it couldn't hurt. "Maybe we need to do the ceiling too," she suggested, pointing toward the attic, and we did. Sitting inside the circle of scarves, we stared into each other's eyes and waited for something to happen. It was silent for a long time.

"I think it worked," Kat announced, yawning. We blew out the candle and tried to go back to sleep. Behind the blackness of my window I thought I heard drums again, beating from far away. Before I could decide if it was just my imagination or branches rattling in the wind, the pictures behind my eyelids faded into dreams.

The next thing I knew it was morning. I threw back the covers and stared at the ceiling. "What do you think made that noise in the attic last night?"

Kat looked like it was no big deal. "Probably just a spirit."

"My Great-Aunt Evelyn's ashes were in an urn in the attic and they spilled," I confided.

"That must be what we heard. Her spirit is angry with someone, so she's haunting the attic." Kat stared at me like this was so obvious I should have thought of it. "Maybe she's trying to get back into the urn. Who spilled her ashes?"

"Gwendolyn didn't say." I looked out the alcove window into the twisted branches of the giant oak. A cool breeze blew between the mountains, and a few dry leaves flew off the tree and sailed across the backyard. Except for the wind, the hills were silent. In the daylight, women wailing and people drumming seemed about as likely as Gwendolyn dancing down the Santa Monica pier in tights and a tutu.

Kat struggled out of her sleeping bag and stood up. "Let's hurry and get dressed so we can get back to the forgotten garden." We put on our clothes and I grabbed my Porta-detective kit, then we ran down the stairs. After gulping down some cereal and juice, we walked past the stream and the willows. Soon we were stepping across the stones toward the gate. "Nine stones," Kat commented.

I was tired of asking what everything meant. I knew nine must be a magic number. We walked into the garden and I felt excitement wash over me as I shared my secret place with my new friend. Knotted gray branches climbed the walls and twisted brown vines covered the ground. "Should we try to clear some of this dead stuff away?" I suggested.

She nodded. "It will help the rest of the garden to grow."

"When I was exploring last week I saw a box of gardening tools behind the stable," I said, turning back toward the gate.

"Excellent. Let's go," Kat said, leading the way. We were running across the yard when Kat stopped suddenly. "Who's that?" she asked in a low voice.

"The stable boy. His name is Carlos. He and his parents live in the guesthouse. They take care of the yard and the animals."

His shirt was off, and sweat shined on his dark skin. Kat stood still and stared at him. I hoped he wouldn't look over and see us. "How old is he?" she whispered.

"Fifteen, I think." I'd never paid much attention to Carlos before, except when he was saddling up the horses and I had to make an excuse not to ride one. But now that Kat was interested, I noticed he had glossy brown hair that needed cutting, a flat stomach, and ropy muscles in his arms. "He doesn't speak the best English."

"What does he speak, Spanish?" Kat asked.

"Yes, mostly Spanish. His mom's Hispanic and his dad's Native American. They're really nice—"

Kat didn't care about Carlos's parents so she talked right over me. "He's half Indian? Interesting. He's super cute. Go get those tools. Maybe he'll notice me."

Walking behind the stable, I picked up the box of tools. As soon as I got back to Kat and set it down, she grabbed my arm tightly. She stared at Carlos with a sly smile on her face. "Introduce us."

Carlos was stabbing piles of hay with a pitchfork and tossing them into the horses' stalls. "Um," I paused, watching him work. "He looks pretty busy right now."

The light went out in Kat's eyes. "Come on, Skylar. He's not that busy." She looked me up and down, like I didn't quite measure up.

I glanced back and forth between my new friend and my aunt's worker. "This box is heavy. I'll introduce you to him later."

Kat put her hands on her hips and looked like she wanted to slap me. "Cross your heart and hope to die?"

I took a step back. "Yes. I promise."

"All right. Let's go."

I felt Kat's eyes boring into my back as we walked across the yard and down the steppingstones. Back in the garden, we snipped dead branches off the bushes and stacked them up. It wasn't long before we were both grunting and sweating in front of a big pile of trimmings. I put on a ratty pair of gloves that were much too big and carried the branches to the woodpile behind the stable.

Panting as I ran back through the gate, I stopped and saw Kat staring at the dirt in the back of the garden. "Sky, quick, come here!" she shouted from the shadowed corner behind the pond. "Look what I found." I ran over to where she was squatting and saw a wooden square half hidden in the dirt. Its corner poked out of the garden floor, teasing us like an unopened invitation. I couldn't wait to figure out what she'd discovered. Bending down, I used my trowel to scrape the earth away from the edges of the wood.

"Be careful, the wood is probably rotten," Kat said.

We gently rubbed away dirt until we revealed the top of a box. A curling design was carved into wood that was caked with mud. The corner of the box looked soft, like it had started to rot in the moist ground. "Who would bury a box back here?" I wondered aloud.

Kat's green eyes shined. "Whoever planted this garden had something important she needed to hide."

"You're right. Let's dig it out and find out what's inside."

We jiggled the damp box back and forth. "I think it's getting loose," she said as we wrestled with it some more. "I hope it isn't locked. We don't want to have to break it open. That would be very bad luck," Kat warned.

We didn't have to worry. After gently scraping all the dirt from around its edges, the box finally came free. It was pretty big, like it could have held a textbook or a hardcover novel. I held it in my hands and Kat slowly opened the lid. We looked into each other's eyes.

The box was empty, except for an old, rusted key.

13
Buried Key

"That key looks super old," Kat said, staring at it.

I picked up the key and turned it over in my hands. "There's a swirling pattern etched into the metal. It's bigger than my diary key but smaller than my house key. What do you think a key this size would unlock?"

"Could be anything. A castle door?"

I shook my head. "Too small." Kat's eyes narrowed. "Someone's secret diary?" I guessed.

"Too boring," she retorted.

"Or maybe not boring at all," I countered. "But they probably wouldn't bury the key. I'll do some investigating and figure it out." Opening my Porta-detective kit, I took out the wax and pressed the key into it. When I peeled off the key, the wax held a perfect copy of the swirling design. "Maybe I can look up old keys on the Internet."

"Good idea. If that doesn't work we can try a locating spell to find the lock. I wonder if there's anything else buried back here," Kat said, looking around.

"Let's keep digging," I suggested, stashing the key in my Porta-detective kit.

After an hour had passed, my legs and back were aching. The sun was directly above us, and Kat pushed sweaty hair out of her eyes. We'd searched the entire garden but didn't dig up anything else that was interesting. "I haven't found anything but weeds," she said, discouraged. We decided to take a break and jump in the pool to cool off, and ran upstairs to put on our bathing suits.

Gwendolyn stood halfway up the staircase, blocking our path. "What were you two doing last night?" she demanded, standing solidly in our way.

"Nothing special," I answered.

Kat looked her right in the eye. "We were trying to cleanse this house of evil," she said clearly. "Excuse us." Gwendolyn looked very surprised and stepped aside, letting us pass.

It happened just like my dad said. *Bullies are really chickens, Skylar. Remember that and gain strength from it.* As soon as we stood up to Gwendolyn she backed down.

We ran down the hallway, closed my bedroom door, and burst out laughing. "Did you see her face?" I giggled. "She looked like you poked her in the eye or something."

"She looked guilty if you ask me," Kat said. "Hide the key before we go swimming."

I pulled open the closet door, planning to put the old metal key inside the hatbox with my diary. I took the top off the third box, picked up the cowboy hat, and gasped.

14
A Perfect Fingerprint

whirled around and looked at Kat. "Someone stole my diary." Her eyes narrowed. "And I think I know exactly who it was."

"Where was your diary?" she demanded, leaning into the closet to look over my shoulder.

"Don't touch anything—we can't disturb the evidence. I have to dust for fingerprints." After unlocking my detective kit I plucked out a bottle of powder, a soft brush, and a roll of clear tape.

"What's all that stuff?" Kat asked.

"Fingerprinting materials," I said briskly, like a detective in an old movie. I wished I had a cup of coffee steaming on the desk in my dimly lit office, and that rain was coming down so hard that it sizzled on the street outside. It made me feel good that Kat was watching me, impressed.

Walking back into the closet, I sprinkled white fingerprinting powder onto the shiny black hatbox surface. "Mm-hmm," I muttered, carefully dusting the excess powder away. "Here's a perfect fingerprint. Hand me a strip of tape please." I pointed at the roll of sticky tape, and she tore off a piece and handed it to me. I pasted it onto the powder and lifted the print, then pressed the tape down onto black construction paper. I pointed back into the kit. "Magnifying glass, please." Kat reached inside my detective kit and passed the glass to me. I examined the print through it. I know what my own fingerprints look like from practicing on myself dozens of times. This one wasn't mine. "Please hand me the evidence envelope in the inside pocket."

Kat dug back into the kit and found the envelope. "Whose fingerprint is this?" she asked, looking at the Case Solution card it was taped to.

"Gwendolyn's."

"How do you know?"

"I captured it myself and labeled it in invisible ink."

"Wow," she said softly.

I examined Gwendolyn's fingerprint through the magnifying glass, comparing it to the new one I had lifted off of the hatbox. There was a pronounced whorl right in the center of each print.

Case Solution:

\# Stolen Diary

Gwendolyn

"It's an exact match."

I filled in the case line on the Solution card: Stolen Diary.

15
Stolen Diary

Kat and I glared at each other as I imagined Gwendolyn breaking into my closet and rooting through my things. Then we marched down the stairs and into the kitchen. My cousin was sitting at the table wolfing down a thick sandwich. "So, Gwendolyn, something seems to be missing from a box in my closet." I stared right at her and raised one eyebrow a notch, waiting for her to deny the theft.

She chewed a huge bite for a long time and smiled. Hunks of bread were lodged between her teeth. "Not your closet," she said matter-of-factly, taking another big bite. Kat shot her a wicked look.

"O-*kay*," I said, drawing out the word, "I put something of mine into the closet in the rose room, and now it's missing. Know anything about a diary?" I tapped my foot smugly, knowing I had positive proof.

"No. But I did see a little book full of retard writing when I was looking for my *hat*," she retorted with her mouth full. Then she laughed, spitting crumbs everywhere.

"You stole it, and I can prove it. You left your fingerprints all over the hatbox. Now where is it?" I demanded, right as my aunt walked in.

"Hello girls," she said cheerfully. Aunt Caroline tapped her fingertips on the counter as she looked at each of our faces. "Everything OK?" She could tell something was definitely wrong.

"Gwendolyn stole my diary," I said, glaring at my cousin.

"What?" Aunt Caroline asked, looking at her daughter.

"Didn't know it was hers. It was in one of our hatboxes, and it looks like a two-year-old scribbled in it." Gwendolyn drummed her fingers on her belly.

Kat smirked. My cousin couldn't tell that it was backward writing.

"Give it back please." Aunt Caroline stared at her, waiting.

Gwendolyn sunk her teeth into the sandwich for another chomp. "Can't," she said, exposing pastrami. "Threw it in the trash."

My cheeks flamed red. "*What* trash?"

"Outside." She jerked her thumb toward the stable and belched. "'Scuse me," she said politely, smiling at her mother. Kat and I ran out the back door, leaving Aunt Caroline apologizing behind us.

I bent over the first trash bin and looked for my diary. It was full of horse manure and it stunk like crazy, but I didn't care and fished around with one hand. Carlos walked over and I tried to remember a few words of Spanish. "*¿Donde esta…?*" I couldn't remember the word for *book*, and I sure didn't know how to say *diary*.

"*¿Esto?*" he asked, holding up my diary. "Is yours?" I nodded. "I think maybe no garbage."

He handed it to me and I smiled gratefully. "*Gracias.*" Kat stared at Carlos and then looked at me hopefully. "Carlos, this is my friend Kat. Kat, this is Carlos."

"Nice to meet you," she said, smiling shyly. I'd never

seen her act like that before.

He nodded at Kat and then turned back to me with a warning in his eyes. "Uh…." I could tell he was trying to think of the English words. "Many crows. At night. No good. *Brujas*," he said, pointing to the hills, and I saw Kat stiffen.

Now someone else was warning me about Shadow Hills. "What's wrong?" I asked. "What's broo-hah?"

Carlos looked at me with worry in his dark eyes. "Just careful, OK?" He turned around to go back to work.

"Wait," I said, grabbing his arm. "Why did you just warn me about the crows?"

He shook his head and didn't answer me. Maybe he didn't know how to explain it in English. Or maybe he just didn't want to say any more. He waited for me to let go of his arm and walked back toward the stable.

"He's unbelievably cute," Kat said, with a determined look on her face.

"Hm," I mumbled, my mind on something more important. Like Googling *black crows* and *bruja* and figuring out what Carlos was trying to warn me about. I looked at the diary in my hand, worried that I wouldn't find a safe place to hide it.

Then Kat startled me. "*Bruja* is Spanish for *witch*," she said, like she'd read my mind. Kat couldn't help looking up at the mountainside. "He knows."

A silent wind blew past us, brushing across my skin like it was carrying secrets.

"I thought I heard drumming last night. What is it? I've heard it before, too."

There. I'd said it. I couldn't take it back, gulp down my

words like medicine and get rid of them.

Kat looked away, like now she was the nervous one.

"You might as well tell me," I said. "I'm a detective. You know I'll figure it out anyway."

She looked down for a second, then met my eyes. "It's Demonia. Carlos must know all about them. He's lived here a long time, right?"

"Long as I can remember. What about Demonia?" *What does Carlos know that he's not telling me?*

"During the full moon they have ceremonies. With sacrifices. You don't want to be anywhere near them when that happens," Kat warned.

"Sac—what kind of sacrifices?" I croaked. My throat suddenly felt like it was coated with dust.

Kat looked down and didn't answer my question. "Wister tries to stop them. Diana said her coven has tried every hex imaginable, banishing and revenge spells, everything they can think of. But Demonia's too powerful." Kat had a funny look on her face. Like she'd already said too much. "Never mind."

Sounds like Wister doesn't only practice white magic, I thought. *And something really bad is happening up in Shadow Hills.*

"Just forget it," Kat said, as we walked across the lawn.

"OK," I agreed. Promising to forget, and knowing I wouldn't.

16
Beautiful Strange Music

We went upstairs and put on our bathing suits. Kat dove into the pool first and raced me to the deep end and back. Then we floated on rafts. I tried to get a tan, and Kat held onto the side of the pool so she could stay in the shade. Her skin was goth-white and she wanted to keep it that way. I noticed that Kat kept looking over at the stables, probably wanting to catch a glimpse of Carlos. Or hoping he'd see her lying on a raft in her bikini. I could really care less about my tan. I kept sneaking glances up into the hills, worrying about what would happen after the sun set and the full moon rose.

After we dried off from swimming we scarfed a quick sandwich and got ready to go to Kat's house. I hid my diary and the rusty key in the old wooden box. We covered it with moist earth from the darkest corner of the garden and topped it with a pile of dead weeds. Neither of us could think of a better hiding place to keep the key safe until we found the matching lock. Then we climbed onto our bikes, headed down the driveway, and raced each other through the neighborhood.

"I need to stop at the souvenir shop next to Trancas Market," Kat called over her shoulder.

"OK. Why?" I shouted as we pedaled down the sidewalk on Pacific Coast Highway.

"They have a little pharmacy. I have to pick up Devon's allergy pills," she said grumpily, standing up on her bike to go faster.

I followed her into the parking lot and we rested our bikes against the wall of the store. The front door was dirty, and a cracked plastic sign on it read: *Malibu Curios & Souvenirs*. A skinny guy wearing stained pants lurked in the back of the store. He had a broom in his hands but he wasn't using it. His pale, stringy hair looked like it hadn't been washed for several days. Kat walked up to a counter littered with scraps of paper.

The clerk walked over to us, limping on one leg. "Help you?" His high-pitched voice sounded like it had never changed. I noticed his nametag read, "Dilbert."

"I'm supposed to pick up my brother's prescription. Devon Feloni."

Dilbert's eyes narrowed. "Feloni?" he asked, and Kat nodded. He glared at her for minute, then limped around the counter and came back with a small bag in his hands. Dilbert took Kat's money and didn't thank her.

We left the store and got back on our bikes. "He wasn't very friendly."

"He's a jerk," Kat said. "I don't know what his problem is. Probably mad at the world that he sounds like a girl." She laughed, pedaling down the street.

By the time we got to her house I was out of breath. I acted like I was winded from the bike ride. The truth was, the thought of meeting Kat's sister was making me nervous.

Kat's house was right on the beach. Its back seemed to poke out of the cliff side. The front of the house was perched high above the sand on what looked like giant stilts. I followed Kat up a steep staircase and through heavy front doors. We passed a marble entryway and walked into a living room with walls made of glass. I looked out at the ocean and felt like we were on a big boat, the water looked so close and so blue.

"Are your parents home?" I asked.

"They're never home. Probably at some party. My mom's an actress so she knows a lot of people," Kat explained. "And my dad just likes to party."

"What movies has your mom been in?"

"No movies, just TV. Soaps." Kat made a face.

"Which one?" I asked, even though I didn't watch them either.

"She was on *The Bold and the Beautiful* for a long time. Now she's on some new one." I could tell Kat was sick of everyone asking about her mom. "Want to meet my brother Devon?"

"Sure," I said, looking around. Her house was eerily quiet, as if it was listening to us. Then a huge wave exploded outside.

"Follow me," Kat said. We climbed a wide staircase and turned down a hall. I heard beautiful strange music coming from behind a bedroom door. It stopped when she knocked.

The door opened slowly and I found myself staring at a smaller version of Kat. Devon had her curly black hair and softer green eyes, but he was short for a ten-year-old and incredibly thin. Sharp cheekbones looked like they were ready to burst through his pale skin. I could see his collarbones poking out from under his T-shirt. "This is my friend Sky," Kat said. "Sky, this is my brother Devon."

He raised one frail hand in a wave. His delicate fingers looked like they would snap like chalk if you pressed on them. "That music was beautiful," I told him. "Were you playing it?"

Devon smiled and nodded as we walked into his bedroom. "Thank you."

A big telescope sat in front of his window, aimed toward the hills on the other side of Pacific Coast Highway. His 'scope looked professional, like one a real scientist would use. When he saw me looking at it, Devon walked over to it casually. Then he rested a finger gently on the eyepiece, lowering it slowly until the other end of the telescope pointed up toward the sky. I wanted to march over to the 'scope, point it back toward Shadow Hills, and look through it to see what he'd been watching.

An astronomy chart hung on the wall between huge fun-house mirrors and posters of rock stars screaming on stage. The first mirror made me look wide and squat, like a fat toad. I turned around, and a mirror on the other side of the room turned me into a pencil-thin giant. "Devon likes his mirrors. He thinks it evens everybody out," Kat explained.

Devon picked up a funny-looking stringed instrument. "Want to hear some more sitar?" I nodded and he began to play another haunting melody.

I was enjoying the music and checking out his posters when Kat said, "We'll see you later Devon. We have things to do."

"What, your witchcraft mumbo jumbo?" He rolled his eyes, just like Kat.

"Careful what you say or we'll put a hex on you," Kat warned. As I followed her out of the room, I couldn't help but notice Devon staring out his window with the same worried look on his face that my aunt sometimes wore. Kat closed his door behind us and led me down the hall.

"This is my room," she said, pulling me inside. There were interesting objects everywhere I looked. Kat grabbed my arm and we walked over to the window. "This is my air quadrant, symbolizing knowledge." Tall, white and whisper-green candles rested on the windowsill next to an incense burner holding fragrant sticks. A bookshelf held an unusual collection of books: *The Learned Arts of Witches & Wizards. Magic Tricks to Impress at Parties. Sleight of Hand and How to Make Objects Disappear. Tabletop Magic. Chemicals that Change the Properties of Matter. The Art of Ventriloquism: How to Throw Your Voice, and Magick Herbs and the Power of Runes*. Bundles of dried herbs were tied over the window, and a long wand carved from wood rested on the sill. It looked like the end of a new tree branch: a sapling that wasn't ready to be cut.

"This quad is fire, for strength and will." She pointed to the fireplace in the opposite wall. Red and orange candles shared the hearth with glazed dishes holding colored rocks and a sword made of stone. It was gray and pitted and looked heavy, like it didn't want you to pick it up.

A deck of playing cards sat in a wooden cradle. "What card games do you know?" I asked.

"Those aren't for games. It's a special deck I use for tricks. I bet kids at school five bucks I can guess their card. Works every time," Kat said proudly. "Want to bet me five dollars I can guess your card?" She held out the deck toward me and laughed when I shook my head. "Good choice." Kat went back into her fire quadrant and put the cards in their holder, then fumbled around for a few seconds before she walked back up to me. "Oh look!" Kat said, reaching for my hair. "You have something shiny right there." She reached her empty hand toward my head, and came away with a polished seashell in her fingers.

"How did you do that?" I asked, touching my hair.

Kat just smiled, enjoying her secret.

On the other side of her room there was an aquarium filled with blue and green fish. Next to the fish tank a round table was covered with glass bowls. Some contained shells and what looked like seawater: cloudy, with particles that had settled at the bottom. Other bowls held pebbles, glitter, and sand. There was a big one filled with blue-tinted water and floating candles. "Water quadrant?"

Kat lit the candles and nodded. "Water for the emotions, and earth for the body." A group of plants sat on the floor, surrounded by decorative rocks. Green, orange, and brown candles rested in unglazed clay pots.

"I love it," I told her, looking forward to redoing my room at home in Santa Monica. When I realized back home was far away from Kat and unlocking the secrets in the forgotten garden, staying at my aunt and uncle's house for the summer didn't seem so bad.

"Thanks," she said. Suddenly I smelled incense. Kat's head turned toward the door. "I bet my sister is getting ready to leave."

Before I had a chance to say anything there was a sharp rap on Kat's door. It flew open without an invitation and her sister stepped into the room.

She looked like someone on the cover of a romance novel. Or the star of a horror movie. Mountains of curling black hair surrounded her beautiful face and petite body. Long, jet-black eyebrows framed expressive hazel eyes. Her thin legs were wrapped in tan tights and she had high-heeled, pointy shoes on her feet. "This is my sister Diana," Kat said.

Diana's blouse changed colors as she moved, shifting from red to pink to gold. She wore a white cape with a gold satin lining. Diana marched over to me and clasped my hand. "And who is this?"

"My friend, Sky."

"Yes," she said mysteriously. "Good." As if she approved of me. "Nice to meet you. Take care of Devon," she told us, preparing to leave. "And here," Diana said, handing a big book to Kat. "I feel you are searching for something. This should help." Diana nodded at me and whisked through the door with her cape billowing out behind her.

17
Book of Shadows

"What's that?" I asked.

"It's her personal *Book of Shadows*," Kat answered. "It's got every kind of spell you can imagine, her recipes for potions and charms, blessings, moon rituals, and talismans. All witches keep one; it's a record of her journey to the next level."

The next level of what? I wondered, but didn't ask. "How did she know we were looking for a lock? Did you tell her about the buried key?" Looking at the thick book resting in Kat's lap, I wished I had an exciting sister like Diana instead of Gwendolyn for a relative.

"I didn't tell her anything. She's psychic. I'm sure she knows we are looking for a lock. Now we just have to find a spell to help us discover where it is." She opened the powerful book and thumbed slowly through its pages. "Here's a good locating spell. But we need to do it outside at midnight during a full moon. Maybe under one of those weeping willow trees?"

"We need to find a different spell. My aunt will never let us do witchcraft in her backyard at midnight."

"OK, how about this one. We have most of what we need already and it doesn't specify any particular time or phase of the moon. Write this down, OK?" I pulled out my pad and copied down the spell as she read from Diana's *Book of Shadows*. "*To locate your lost or stolen property, fill a chalice with blessed water. Then drop something symbolic of the four elements into the chalice, and swirl the water* deosil."

"What's *dee-oh-sill* and how do you spell it?"

"Clockwise, and d-e-o-s-i-l."

"OK. Then what?"

"Finally, drop in a feather from a rescued bird, and let it spin in the swirling water until it stops of its own accord. It will point in the direction of the missing item."

I kept scribbling down the instructions. "It's not exactly going to lead us right to it, but it's a start," I said, wishing I had brought my detective kit.

Kat smiled at me. "Exactly. Now we just need the feather."

"How are we going to find a rescued bird?" I stopped writing and frowned. "And do we pluck its feather?" I didn't like the sound of that at all.

"We'll find out when we're ready and we'll know when we're sure," Kat said, quoting her sister.

It didn't take long.

18
Witches in Disguise

After I rode home from Kat's we ate dinner, and then Aunt Caroline suggested that Gwendolyn and I play a game together. "OK," I said, thinking I'd rather hop down the halls of Malibu Middle in my bra and underwear.

"I'm not in the mood," Gwendolyn said, and for once I agreed with her. I looked at my aunt and shrugged.

"OK then, let's see what's on Discovery." She marched us into the den and my uncle disappeared up the stairs. We watched a half-hour documentary on dolphins before Aunt Caroline finally let me go to my room.

I walked upstairs, wondering if I would have to bury my latest art project in the earth with the rusted key and my diary to keep it safe from my cousin, the thief. Turning down the hall, I heard a loud whirring sound. My uncle crouched on the floor in front of my door, working on the handle. He wore an old pair of jeans and casual shoes with spongy soles. "Hi Uncle Jim. Um, what are you doing?"

He rattled my door handle and nodded in satisfaction. Then my uncle stood up, brushed sawdust off of his pants, and handed me a key. "Practicing my rusty handyman skills," he said with a smile. "I heard about your diary, and I'm very sorry," he said, shaking his head. "We thought you deserved more privacy than that, so I changed the handle on your door to one that locks. You are the only one with the key, so don't lose it."

"Thanks, that was really nice of you. And don't worry, I won't lose it," I said, planning to keep the key inside the leather pouch with my amulet.

"Gwendolyn is being punished. She's grounded for two weeks with no Internet or telephone privileges. Again, I apologize for her behavior. That was inexcusable. Good night," he said, giving me a quick pat on the shoulder and disappearing down the hall.

Walking into my bedroom, I tested the lock on the door and whispered, "*Yes.*" Now I didn't have to worry about hiding my art projects or burying my diary in the forgotten garden. I couldn't wait to tell Kat that my amulet had worked again. Sure, Gwendolyn breaking into my closet and stealing my stuff had something to do with it, but my uncle could have just grounded her. He didn't have to install a lock on my door. Talk about *protection from evil.* Now I could keep my diary in my room where it belonged, and I could write in it whenever I felt like it.

When it got late enough that I figured my aunt and uncle had gone to sleep, I grabbed my Porta-detective kit and tiptoed down the stairs. Sneaking the sliding glass door open, I crept out into the yard, looking back at the house. The kitchen was dark, but the light was on in my aunt and uncle's bedroom. Their blinds were closed. I was pretty sure no one was watching me.

My heart beating hard, I ran across the uneven backyard, carefully avoiding the stream. The air blowing by my face felt cool and moist. Waves crashed across the rocks and sand, blocks away and far below. When I got closer to the pines I stared up through them past the garden. Way up in the hills a ring of red light flickered, glowing like embers. A moment later there was nothing there. The moon was a silver sliver.

Sneaking through the gate, I walked quickly to the back of the garden. After brushing the leaves and dirt off the top of the buried box, I opened the lid. *Good.* It was still there. Leaving the rusty key, I plucked out my diary, set the box back in its hole, and covered it up.

Just then the drumming started up in Shadow Hills. The garden walls were so tall that I couldn't see over them. I imagined Demonia dancing around a ring of fire and drinking well water, and goose bumps rose on my arms. Carlos had tried to warn me. "Many crows. At night. No good. *Brujas.*"

I had to get back to the safety of my room.

The rusty gate slammed behind me, much louder than I wanted it to. I raced across the stones and through the dark yard, hoping I would make it to the kitchen door before I felt cold fingers on the back of my neck.

The slider stuck, and for a panicked minute I thought I'd gotten locked out. But after a little jiggling I got it open and sped up to my room, quiet as I could be. Kneeling on the window seat, I put my Super-Zoom binoculars up to the window and stared out into the blackness. It stayed dark for so long that I started to wonder if I'd seen red lights flickering after all. Was my imagination tricking me? I didn't think it was.

I opened my diary and printed my entry backward:

Dear Diary,

This summer has been very strange so far. Kat is teaching me all sorts of cool stuff about magic and witchcraft. Things mom and dad always told me were baloney. But strange things keep happening that I can't logically explain. Like as soon as we did the spell to make my amulet powerful, Gwendolyn tried to barge into my room, but she couldn't open the door. And it wasn't even locked! Maybe she was just yanking the handle to bug us. But maybe she really was trying to get in. Supposedly there's a coven called Demonia that does black magic in the hills behind Gwendolyn's house. I'm not sure if I believe in this stuff or not. Need to investigate further.

Kat and I were exploring the forgotten garden and we found a rusty old key buried inside a box. I can't wait to find out what it unlocks!

The only thing that sucks is mom and dad haven't even called me. Their emails and texts just warn me to be good and mind Aunt C and Uncle J or brag about their trip. They didn't even ask me if I was having fun or say they miss me. I guess they are VERY BUSY exploring Europe.

My eyes started to sting as I thought about my parents completely forgetting about me while they had fun in some faraway country. Then the page got so blurry I couldn't see it anymore. I locked my diary and stashed it under my mattress.

To get my mind off my mom and dad, I Googled *black crows* and *bruja*. Nothing came up except lots of posts about the band The Black Crowes. But when I tried *black crows and witch* it was a different story.

Black crows and ravens can be witches in disguise. They

are considered messengers of the gods, and are thought to be birds of omen and prophecy. Because of his intelligence and cunning, the crow is also seen as a trickster. Many believed that fairies turn into crows in order to cause mischief.

"Crows can be witches in disguise," I whispered, wondering what else Carlos knew, and wasn't saying. What was really going on in the hills behind my aunt's house, making her nervous as she stared out the window? After that I got into bed, but it took a long time to get to sleep. Every time I was about to fade, I thought about Devon watching Shadow Hills through his telescope, and wondered what he'd seen.

I dreamed about crows flying past the moon, and turning into witches on broomsticks.

19
The Hidden Staircase

Later that night I woke up suddenly, hearing a strange noise. While I waited for my eyes to adjust to the dark, I heard it again: a soft clunking sound over my head. I looked at the clock on my bedside table: 12:07.

The witching hour had started.

I looked out the window. The hillside was dark and quiet.

Then another muffled thump sounded from the room above mine. I didn't believe in ghosts or zombies. But something or someone was definitely moving around up there. I could just hear my dad: "Skylar, get serious. Nobody's roaming around in the attic."

Thump. De-bump. *Sure, Dad. Explain that.*

If only I had the proper equipment, I would march right up those stairs and confront whatever was up there. Suddenly I was lost in a fantasy, armed with an arsenal of weapons, ready to conquer any enemy:

Grandpa's bulletproof vest covered my entire chest and stomach. Pulling my arms through thick leather straps, I lifted a heavy oxygen tank onto my back and placed its mask over my mouth and nose. My safety goggles had thick plastic lenses. They were built to withstand blinding light, flying particles from an explosion, burning gasses, and animal claws or fangs. I stepped into tall rubber boots, pulling on matching gloves and a metal helmet. The digital selector on my gun had buttons for three types of enemies: human, animal, and ghoul. If I got attacked in the attic, my opponent would receive a shower of bullets, a dart full of sedative, or poison vapor that would turn the un-dead into instant mist. Ready for anything, I headed for the hidden staircase.

Huddling under my covers, I remembered Aunt Caroline's warning: "Stay out of the attic." I pictured her fingers moving while she tried to think of a reason why I shouldn't go up there. Then I heard a new noise, which was even more horrifying. It sounded like somebody up in the attic was crying. It was a high-pitched weeping sound, and it made my blood freeze to hear it. Who or what was trapped up there?

I knew what Kat would say: "Duh. Evelyn's ghost is haunting the attic where her ashes spilled." I rolled over and put the pillow over my ear, trying to force myself to go back to sleep.

Yeah, right.

My curiosity beat my fear. I had to see if I could still hear anything, and tossed the pillow aside. The rose room was dimly lit by the moonlight coming through the bay window. A moment later I heard another feeble cry. Detective Skylar took over and I threw the covers back. This definitely needed investigating, and it could not wait until morning. I never imagined I would find the courage to sneak into the attic at midnight by myself.

Creeping out of bed, I grabbed the flashlight from my detective kit. With my heart pounding, I slipped three sacred stones into the pocket of my bathrobe for luck. In case there was someone lurking around the attic I took my laser pointer too, wishing I had a weapon that would really protect me.

Unarmed, I headed for the hidden staircase. I turned on my flashlight and pointed its beam down the dark hallway. Maybe my aunt or uncle would come out and catch me, sending me back to the safety of my room. I was so nervous my knees felt wobbly. Seeing Gwendolyn would have even been OK.

No one came.

Opening the door to the hidden stairway, I took a deep breath and put my foot on the first step. The crying got a little louder and I heard a soft thumping sound. The staircase was a lot shorter than I would have liked. In no time at all I was standing in front of the attic door, shining my light on the old knob. Slowly I pushed open the door.

Closing it quietly behind me, I took shallow breaths while my eyes adjusted to the gloom. "OK, Sky, you've got this," I whispered, aiming my flashlight around the attic. The beam danced off a padlocked trunk and stacks of boxes and bundles. Some of the cartons towered higher than my head. Was someone hiding behind them, ready to jump out and grab me? I tiptoed sideways and shined the light behind the tallest pile.

No one was there.

Trying not to think about Great-Aunt Evelyn's ashes, I stepped forward and heard it again: a muffled thump followed by a sorrowful cry. I turned to my right. A small window was backlit by the moonlight outside. That's when I saw it.

"Oh no," I cried. A skinny blue jay was sitting on the windowsill. I wondered how long it had been trapped in the attic without anything to eat or drink. "It's you that's been making the clunking noises and crying."

The bird was so weak that she didn't try to fly away as I crept over to her. She just fluttered to the ground as I jiggled the window open. As fresh air filled the stuffy attic, I backed away slowly so she wouldn't be afraid. With two determined flaps of her wings she managed to get onto the sill, cocking her head toward the window. The twisted oak tree was right outside, and she hopped off the windowsill onto one of its boughs. The blue jay immediately started to peck at the branch beneath her feet. I hoped she'd found some seeds or bugs to eat.

"You're free now," I said. After shutting the attic window, I looked around and remembered where I was. The chunky shapes of my great-aunt's belongings loomed in the dark as I shined my flashlight on the floor. Thankfully, there weren't any ashes flying around as I'd imagined. But I watched my feet very carefully so I wouldn't step in a pile of Evelyn's "things" as I tiptoed toward the door.

When I reached the doorway I gasped out loud. Something amazing was sitting on the floor as if it was waiting for me to find it. Chills ran through my body and I felt the hair rise up on the back of my neck. I picked it up and crept down the hidden staircase. Then I tiptoed down the hall to my room to examine my find. The house was totally quiet, so I turned on my bedside lamp.

And stared in wonder at the feather from the bird I had just rescued.

20
Feather from a Rescued Bird

I took the blue feather to school the next day, and absolutely could not wait for Kat to get to class. The bell rang and she still wasn't there. I was about to jump out of my skin with disappointment when the door opened. She stuck her head in with a sheepish smile on her face and hurried to her chair.

"I overslept," Kat whispered. "I was up all night reading Diana's *Book of Shadows*. You are not going to believe what we are going to do."

"And you are not going to believe—this!" I said, whipping out my feather.

Her eyes widened and her mouth fell open. "Is that—?"

"Yes. I rescued this poor little blue jay last night. She was stuck in the attic for who knows how long. Probably flew in through the vent, and that's what was clunking around up there and crying. She was flying into things trying to escape. It wasn't Great-Aunt Evelyn's spirit after all. So now we can finish the spell and get another clue to figure out what the key unlocks."

"Girls, *please*," Miss Yamato said, looking sternly at us. Today her new skirt and jacket were dark red and a little too big, like she expected to grow into them. Kat and I couldn't wait for the break to start so we could fill each other in. Finally it was 10:20, and we walked across the grass together, looking at the blue-green ocean.

Kat started. "First we need to do the locating spell

104

and find the lock that matches the rusted key. We need to unlock that box, container, or door, and see what's inside. It could help us with our next spell." She waited for me to ask.

"What's our next spell?"

Kat lowered her voice. "There's a whole section in Diana's *Book of Shadows* on garden witchery. It tells how to prepare the earth, and in which phase of the moon we need to plant for the best results. Then, when we have our altar all prepared and the garden is ready," Kat looked over her shoulder to make sure no one could hear her, then clutched my arm, "we are going to grow gems."

"Grow *what*?" There was no way I heard her right.

Kat's eyes gleamed. "*Gems*. You know, rubies, emeralds, sapphires? Gems! I copied all the instructions for the spell last night. That's why I was up so late; I'm not sure when Diana will need her book back."

"This sounds crazy," I said.

But two days ago, so did finding a feather from a rescued bird. And I held one in my hand.

21
The Missing Lock Spell

The next morning on the bus Rudy Dean waved me over. "Yo, new girl." He said it like we'd been friends forever and I wasn't the new girl at all. He scooted over as much as he could, trying to make room for me.

I sat down next to him and pointed at his sketchpad. "Let's see." He opened it up and showed me his latest drawing: fairies flying around the head of a dragon. "That's sick."

"Thanks," he said, frowning at it like he thought it sucked. "Nowhere near done."

We turned onto Pacific Coast Highway and I looked at the dark blue ocean welling up past the sand. A wave broke, spraying foam. "What are you and Andy doing for your project?"

Rudy laughed. "Good question. That a funny dude."

"It was nice of you to partner up with him."

Rudy looked at me with his eyebrows pulled down. "Why? 'Cause dude's deaf?"

"Well, yeah. I guess," I said, feeling small. "Like, isn't it hard to work out what your project's going to be?"

"No. Interpreter gets it all translated. Just Andy wants to make a model of this *war*, like my drawings, you know? Angels against demons and all that? But I'm like, Dude!" He mimed a bad imitation of sign language. "We got like pipe cleaners and pencils to work with. You crazy?" He laughed and so did I.

"Sounds ambitious."

"Sounds impossible," he said, riffling the corner of his sketchpad with his thumb.

The bus rounded a curve in the coastline. Across the street from the ocean I saw Shadow Hills rising up behind the houses and shops. "Hey Rudy, can I ask you something?" He nodded once. "I've heard rumors about things happening up in Shadow Hills at night. Evil things." Rudy frowned. "Uh, do you know what really goes on up there?"

He looked past me toward the window on the opposite side of the bus. "Nothin' good, that's for sure." The coast curved again and Shadow Hills were behind us now.

"Like what?"

"Don't go messing around up there, new girl." I expected him to add, *if you know what's good for you.*

"Why not?" I pressed.

"Look," he said, and now he sounded impatient. "I heard there's druggies living in tents up there who'll rob you blind. Or kidnap you. I also heard Devil worshippers, but I don't believe in that nonsense." Rudy frowned. "Best to just stay out of there, period."

The bus pulled over to the curb and lurched to a stop. I waited for Rudy to continue but he was finished talking and stood up. He followed me into the aisle and we waited for the kids ahead of us to get off.

"'Scuse me," Gwendolyn said loudly, right behind us.

Rudy Dean turned around very slowly and scowled at Gwendolyn. The smirk fell right off her face. "You in a big hurry or something?" he said, not moving. Gwendolyn actually seemed to shrink right in front of my eyes. Rudy didn't budge. Kids squeezed around Gwendolyn and past Rudy and me to get off the bus, but he held her still with his dark stare. The bus cleared out and there was no one in front of us anymore. "Bus on fire?" He switched his sketchpad to his other hand and glared at my cousin.

Gwendolyn shook her head nervously. I smiled.

Rudy made her wait another couple of seconds. "OK then. Ready, new girl?" he said, holding out his arm like he was my date at the prom. I put my hand on it and we walked casually off the bus with Gwendolyn following silently behind.

Right after school Kat and I headed for the forgotten garden. We carried ingredients for the locating spell and items that symbolized the four elements. The feather from the rescued bird was tucked inside an evidence envelope with a mussel shell. I had some knotted rope, our sword, and the wand. Kat carried a plastic pitcher, a packet of salt, matches, and a purple candle. We stopped at the stream and let water trickle into the pitcher. Then we hopped across the stones, passed through the rusty gate, and filled the chalice. After circling it with the rope, we were ready to perform the spell to help us find the missing lock.

I'd never believed in magic before, but I was starting to get a tingling feeling. A locating spell couldn't actually work. *Could it?*

Kat dropped a sacred stone into the chalice to represent earth. I tossed in some sage and jasmine for air, and added the mussel shell for water. She lit the candle and splashed some purple wax into the water for fire. Then we sat down next to each other on the old stool. Kat handed me the wand, and I stirred the water clockwise while she held the burning candle. When the water was moving fairly quickly, I dropped in the feather from the rescued bird. Then we recited the spell.

"Feather from a rescued bird, in deosil swirling water bind; the correct direction it will point, and the missing item I shall find."

A bank of fog passed in front of the sun. June gloom. All of a sudden the garden was shrouded in shadow. We watched quietly as the feather spun around and around, finally coming to a complete stop. Kat touched my arm and we turned around and looked up at the small dark window. "You see where it's pointing, don't you?"

I nodded. "The rusted key opens something that's locked up in the attic."

A chilly breeze blew into the garden. Flowers bent on their stems, and the pile of weeds flew off the wooden box. Kat and I stared at each other. "I told you the vibrations are incredible in here," she whispered. "It's like there's a spirit that's speaking to us."

I found an old hose coiled in the corner hidden beneath big nasturtium leaves. "Hold this over the pond," I said, handing it to Kat. After tugging on the handle, some brownish water squirted out of the hose. "Let it run for a minute and it will probably get clearer." Sure enough, the murky water got lighter and lighter and soon it was coming out clear. After we filled the pond, we spent the rest of the afternoon pulling weeds and clearing out more dead branches. We watered whatever was still alive, and tried to figure out how we could sneak into the attic to search for the missing lock.

Late in the afternoon a chilly ocean breeze blew into the garden. Kat looked at me and grinned. "Look around," she said with satisfaction. "It's starting to look like a genuine magic garden."

"We made it our own sacred place." A creepy feeling started to come over me as I looked into the shadowed corners. "The doorway. Like you said."

Kat nodded. "To another dimension."

Then the wind blew harder and the feather began to move. It spun around and around, finally coming to a stop. It pointed toward the gate. I looked at Kat and her eyes narrowed.

We heard footsteps coming across the steppingstones.

22
The Easiest Thing to Steal

Kat turned toward the gate and drew huge stars in the air with the sword. I blew out the candle as we heard Aunt Caroline shout, "Gwendolyn? *Gwendolyn!*"

"Oh no," Kat cried, her green eyes fierce. "Your cousin can't find out that we've turned the forgotten garden into a sacred place; that will ruin *everything.*"

"I don't want my aunt seeing it either," I said as Kat tossed jasmine branches and sage toward the gate. Then she pointed her ring finger at it and made the sign of the pentacle. Like that could really keep my cousin or my aunt from barging into the garden. I held my breath, sure that any second their voices would grow louder and the gate would swing open. Gwendolyn would point at the chalice and laugh, making fun of the circle of rope surrounding it.

But as I stared at Kat's angry face, the footsteps retreated. "That was close," I whispered.

"Too close," Kat answered. "We have to do something right away."

"What should we do?" I had Gwendolyn's fingerprints on file, proving she had stolen my diary. But that wasn't exactly the crime of the century.

"We'll do an incantation to render Gwendolyn harmless."

"A what?"

Kat looked at me like I was four years old. "A spell."

111

Relying on witchcraft didn't make me feel very confident. "Do you know one that actually works?"

Kat ignored the doubtful look on my face. "I'll ask my sister."

I took a breath. "This is white magic, right?"

"Relax. It's nothing evil." Kat looked at me like I was annoying. "Anyway, I know one thing for sure: we'll need something personal of Gwendolyn's."

"That's easy. What should I get?"

"Hair out of her brush is the easiest thing to steal."

"That's gross."

Kat stared at me with her hands on her hips.

"Oh all right, I'll get some."

"We need to do the incantation before we try to get into the attic to look for the missing lock," she said.

"Good idea. Aunt Caroline already told me to stay out of the attic. So we need to sneak up there when she isn't home. We don't want to have to worry about Gwendolyn spying on us too."

"Get the hair tonight and we'll do the spell after school tomorrow."

At that point I still thought witchcraft was probably fake, and that casting spells was just for fun. I had no idea how dangerous the incantation would prove to be.

23
Incantation

Kat came over after school the next day. Rosa was vacuuming downstairs, and my aunt and uncle were both at work. After checking in from the house phone, we crept down the hall to my bedroom. I hoped Gwendolyn wouldn't hear us and come galloping out of her room for a confrontation.

"What did you steal?" Kat asked with her eyes shining. I pulled out the envelope containing the frizzy hair I'd taken from Gwendolyn's brush, and held it open. Kat looked inside, giving me a sly smile and a quick nod.

I locked my bedroom door and led the way outside. When we got to the garden Kat walked through the gate first and cried, "Sky, look." A pair of ducks floated gracefully on the pond.

"It sure didn't take very long for them to find the water."

"Can we get something to feed them?" she asked.

"Do you think they would eat oats?"

"Probably."

"There's a ton of them in the stable." I led the way through the pines and we crossed the lawn.

Her eyes lit up. "Is Carlos working today?"

His golden retriever raced across the grass, wearing a red bandana around its neck instead of a collar. He spun around suddenly and looked at us, his long pink tongue hanging out of the corner of his mouth. "Well yeah, Carlos lives in the guest house. He's in charge of the horses

and my cousin's goats. He's probably working in the stable."

"Let's go!" Her smile was so intense it was scary. We
walked past the pool and Kat fluffed her hair. She reached
into the pocket of her jeans and pulled out a tube of
lip-gloss, put some on, and handed it to me. "It's choco-
late-mint flavored. Want some?"

I wasn't allowed to wear makeup yet. But I figured
if my parents didn't care enough to take me to Europe
with them, it was too bad if I wore makeup behind their
backs. Besides, it was just clear gloss. It wasn't like I got a
tattoo. I pictured my mom lifting her wineglass in a fancy
French restaurant, toasting my dad for taking her on such
a wonderful trip. They obviously weren't worrying about
what I was doing in Malibu. "Sure," I said, grabbing the
lip gloss and smearing it across my lips. Handing the tube
back to Kat, I rubbed my sticky lips together. It smelled a
lot better than it tasted.

Sure enough, Carlos was in the stable brushing a
sweet horse named Brownie. According to the house
rules I wasn't supposed to go inside the stable without
an adult present. But I felt like breaking the rules, so we
walked inside. It smelled like animals and grassy hay.

"Hi Carlos," Kat said, giving him a flirty smile.

"*Hola*. Hallo Skylar." He glanced past us through
the shadows and looked outside. I followed his eyes and
realized he was staring at Gwendolyn's goat pen with his
eyebrows scrunched.

"What's wrong?" I asked, stepping closer to him.

Kat got a strange look on her face, like she wanted to
elbow me out of the way and pounce on him. She walked

forward and stood slightly in front of me. "Yeah, Carlos, what's up?" she asked, touching his arm.

He backed up a little, so Kat took another step closer to him. "*Nada*," he said, and went back to grooming the horses.

Turning around, I walked over to the bin and grabbed a handful of oats. When Kat heard me cross the stable, she followed me and took some too. The big white horse, Lightning, stomped her foot and snorted and I jumped. Kat noticed and laughed. She watched Carlos for another minute before we walked back outside. "He's too cute," she said, looking at me for a reaction.

"I guess."

Kat frowned at me. "You don't think so?"

"He's just been around for so long he's like another cousin."

"OK good." Kat smiled, but I saw the warning in her eyes. "So you'll keep your hands off him."

Back in the garden, we tossed oats to the ducks and watched them snap them up. Then Kat announced, "It's time to do the spell. Let's do it under a weeping willow." We walked out of the garden and passed the stream. "This thick one makes a perfect circle." Parting graceful willow branches, we crawled into the shadows.

Long skinny leaves made a moist green igloo all around us. We sat down on the damp earth next to the trunk. Kat lit the candles, and then looked at me very seriously. "You do believe in magic, right? Because if you don't…." she trailed off, like we were little kids and she was about to pick up her toys and go home.

"I'm not sure," I admitted. "I guess I just don't understand how it could work."

Kat looked at me intensely. Halfway between mad and excited. "OK. I'll prove it to you. Hold your hands up, palms facing each other, about half an inch apart. You'll feel your energy arc back and forth."

I held up my hands with my palms facing each other, and brought them slowly together. When they were half an inch apart, I almost fell over. The shock must have showed on my face.

"Feel that?" she said excitedly. "You just created an electromagnetic field."

OMG, I thought. I *did* feel it.

"Everything around us has positive or negative energy. You just disrupted its natural flow."

I quickly dropped my hands into my lap. This was amazing. I couldn't wait to hear more. "Go on."

"We all radiate energy. When you concentrate your energy and learn to use it, you can submit another person to your will. Make them do what you want. Make them disappear, if you want. It's all energy," she said simply. "You felt it."

"Yeah I did." I faced my palms toward each other to be sure. *And felt my own energy again.*

Kat looked at me like she was calculating something. "OK," she leaned forward like she was about to tell me a juicy secret. "I'll give you a demonstration. I'm going to use positive energy to control your body."

No way, I thought, pressing my hands against the garden floor, ready to stop Kat from controlling my body. There was no way she could make it do something I didn't want it to do—was there? "OK, go ahead," I challenged her.

"Um," Kat touched her chin and looked up into the tree like she was thinking about what she should make me do. "Stick out your right foot and make clockwise circles with it."

"Deosil?" I smiled.

"Deosil." Kat nodded as I stuck out my foot and turned it in circles. "I will now make it change direction."

"Yeah right," I said, spinning my foot around.

She stared at it and her eyes softened as if they were blurring. Kat pointed her index finger and rotated it, following the direction of my foot. "Deosil spin, heed my call, direction change, cast a pall." Kat looked at me. Her finger stopped moving. "Draw a 6 in the air with your right hand. I now command your foot to spin counterclockwise."

I waved a 6 in the air as Kat spun her index finger in the opposite direction.

To my horror my foot followed. It circled counterclockwise—*against my will*. My own body had betrayed me. I put my leg down and leaned toward her, my heart pounding. "How did you do that?" I stomped my feet against the earth, making sure they were both back under my control.

Kat shrugged casually. "Used my energy. That's the basis of personal magic. Concentrating and controlling your energy, then sending it to do your bidding. Here. Hold your hands up facing mine."

After being unable to control my own foot, I was afraid to hold up my hands. But Kat gave me her signature stare so I held them up. We faced palms, an inch apart. I felt her energy. It was even stronger than my own. Electricity crackled between our hands like my hair getting staticky on a windy day. "See? We just created energy, Sky. That's what magic *is*. You create energy, and then you channel it using your mind and will."

This made sense. My foot had changed direction against my will. *Kat was able to control my body with her mind.*

What we were about to do suddenly seemed very serious. I opened the envelope full of Gwendolyn's hair and looked at it. Kat stuck her hand out impatiently until I gave her the envelope. "What we need to do first is called grounding. Empty your mind of all thoughts." I tried, but I was too curious about what was coming next and my mind wouldn't empty. "When your mind is at peace, picture a root—like a tree root, that starts at the top of your head, runs down your spine and straight down into the earth. This is the pathway that will allow your spirit to return to your body after we perform the spell."

I tried not to laugh as I pictured a root cementing my butt to the ground. I wasn't sure if I felt like laughing because it was funny, or because Kat had started to scare me.

"Now picture a ray of golden light coming up from the earth, through the root, and into your body. Then back down into the earth, making you one with the universe. This is your passageway back to the present." The candlelight glimmered, casting wavering shadows onto the leafy walls. Suddenly I could see and feel golden light rising out of the ground and into my body. Taking a deep breath, I felt a cold, electric rush come up through the garden floor. It warmed as it flowed through my stomach and climbed up my spine, finally heating my face.

"It is time for the incantation," Kat whispered as a breeze whistled through the weeping willow branches. "First we have to imagine the purpose of the spell and picture a successful outcome."

"The purpose is to keep Gwendolyn far away from us." I pressed my palms against the moist earth again. The solid ground beneath my fingertips felt safe and reassuring.

"Yes, and to render her harmless. We want to weaken her powers, in case she is an evil spirit. Ready?" I nodded. "I am going to slowly feed her hair into the flame. As it burns, we have to imagine Gwendolyn getting weaker and weaker, smaller and smaller, until she disappears."

I giggled. "I should have gotten a lot more hair."

"Sky, be serious."

"Sorry."

I imagined the golden light grounding me to the earth as Kat picked the ball of frizzy hair out of the envelope. She held it over the purple candle. "As her body burns, her power turns, from strong to weak." The hairball caught on fire and Kat quickly dropped it on the ground. I pictured Gwendolyn shrinking away to nothing as her hair sputtered and sparked.

"That stinks."

Kat looked at me like I had spinach stuck in my teeth. "Shh. Picture Gwendolyn losing all her power."

"I am."

"Repeat the spell."

Kat tipped the candle down and relit the hairball. We chanted the spell over and over as my cousin's hair fizzled into ash. "As her body burns, her power turns, from strong to weak."

"Now picture the golden light coming back out of the earth and into your body, and your spirit will return with it." Kat blew out the candle and the tree cave grew dark. I closed my eyes and felt a burst of energy flow through me as my spirit returned to my body. An eerie feeling came over me as I wondered where it had been. I wiggled my fingers and shook my head to make sure I was all the way back into reality. Kat picked up the candles and I grabbed the matches. We both stood up and were nose-to-nose inside the branches of the weeping willow.

"How long do you think it will take for the spell to work?" I asked.

"I have no idea. But we'll know when we're sure."

We found out soon enough that it had started to work immediately. Much more powerfully than I had wanted it to.

After spending the next afternoon trimming the last dead branches and taking them to the woodpile, Kat and I walked back into the house. My aunt was standing over the stove stirring a big pot of soup.

"Hello girls," she said. "Stay away from Gwendolyn."

Kat and I stared at each other, our eyes widening. Fortunately Aunt Caroline's back was turned so she didn't see the guilty look on our faces.

"Why?" I asked nervously. "Is something wrong?"

"She doesn't look well, and she feels very weak. I'm making chicken soup, if either of you would like a bowl."

My face flushed and my skin prickled. I elbowed Kat

and mouthed, "*Weak.*"

Kat smiled in satisfaction. "No thank you, I'm not hungry. It's time for me to go now."

I walked her to the door, and we stopped and faced each other in the entryway. "This is really scary," I admitted. "What if she gets really sick, or—"

"Or what?" Kat looked at me like I had to be kidding. She had the same gleam in her eye that had made me nervous on the first day of school.

"What if something major happens to her?" I whispered, opening the door. Even if Gwendolyn was the biggest bully on earth, there was no way I wanted something terrible to happen to my cousin.

"Nothing crazy bad's gonna happen," Kat said casually. "But it's out of our hands now anyway." She shrugged and threw one leg over her bike, like she couldn't care less if something horrible happened to Gwendolyn. "See you tomorrow."

I shut the door and looked up through the spider webs into the clouds with a sickening feeling squeezing my stomach.

24
Trapped in the Attic

Friday morning I hurried down the stairs, hoping to catch a glimpse of Gwendolyn before I left for school. Aunt Caroline sat at the kitchen table looking stressed. "Morning," I said casually. "How's Gwendolyn feeling?"

"Not well at all. I'm trying to get her in to see the doctor."

Gulp.

"Is that why you aren't at work?" I asked.

My aunt tip-tapped her fingers against her jaw and nodded.

"What's wrong with her?" I was starting to worry that the incantation might have worked just a little too well.

"We aren't sure yet. Hopefully it's just the flu. She still feels very sick and weak." I flinched again at the sound of the word.

My dad always told me that things like witchcraft were phony. There was no such thing as magic, and spells and incantations were make-believe. He obviously had never seen anything like what Kat was able to conjure up. "I'm late for school. Hope she feels better," I said, hurrying toward the door. I jumped on my bike and pedaled as fast as I could toward Malibu Middle School.

Every neighbor's driveway was like a marker I had to pass. School felt like it was miles and miles away. When the fenced-in buildings finally came into view, I felt like a runner who spotted the finish line. Hurrying into the classroom, I was relieved to find Kat there ahead of me. I dove into my seat. "Gwendolyn's really weak and sick. My aunt stayed home from work to take her to the doctor." I stared at Kat, trying not to squirm while I waited for her reaction.

Kat looked at me like I'd just spoken in Chinese. "So? This is what we wanted, right?"

"I wanted her to leave us alone. I didn't want to kill her," I whispered.

"Calm down, she's not dead." Kat rolled her eyes. "Wait and see what the doctor says before you panic." She dug a mirror out of her purse and smeared on a thick coat of lip gloss.

"Kat. I feel so guilty." I dragged my hand through my hair. "I'm thinking about telling my aunt what we did."

She glared at me and her expression turned ugly. "Don't you *dare*."

After school I stashed my bike in the garage and walked into the house. I checked in with my aunt, went up to my room, and locked myself in. Curling up on the alcove seat, I opened my diary and wrote in it backward:

Dear Diary,

Kat and I did an incantation yesterday to weaken Gwendolyn's powers. Now she's sick and I feel awful. Kat warned me not to confess but Aunt Caroline will be furious if she finds out we cast a spell on her daughter. Not to mention we possibly made her get sick and then I didn't do anything to undo the spell. But Kat will never speak to me again if I tell. Either way I'm going to make someone really mad.

I wish I could talk to my mom. She'd understand and tell me the right thing to do. If I told Dad about the witchcraft he'd tell me Kat really has me fooled, and shake his head. Devon is Kat's brother and he even thinks it's all hocus pocus. But if there really is a chance that I made Gwendolyn sick, I should tell someone, shouldn't I?

I stared out the window into the twisted oak tree, wondering what to do.

Who deserved my loyalty? A family member who had bullied me since we were kids? Or a new friend who I wasn't sure I could really trust?

A skinny blue jay sat on a branch, staring at me. The way she cocked her head seemed familiar. Suddenly I realized it was the bird I had rescued from the attic. I gently raised the window and stuck my head outside. The fresh air felt smooth against my face. "Hey, little one, are you feeling better?"

The blue jay tilted her head to the other side. Then she looked up at the attic window and back at me, like she was trying to tell me something.

"You don't want to go back into the attic, do you?" I asked, and then I got goose bumps. The rescued bird stared quietly at me. "You want *me* to go back up there, don't you?" She looked into my eyes as if she agreed, and then soared off toward Shadow Hills.

I closed my diary and poked my head out into the hall. Aunt Caroline was still at the doctor's office with Gwendolyn. My uncle wouldn't be home from work for another hour. I pictured the feather swirling through the water in the chalice and pointing to the attic window. This was the perfect opportunity to find the lock that matched the rusted key. Locking the door behind me, I grabbed my Porta-detective kit. Listening for any sound of my aunt's car coming up the drive, I tore across the backyard, heading for the forgotten garden.

After brushing the dirt and weeds off the top of the old wooden box, I opened it and grabbed the key. I popped it into my kit so I wouldn't drop it running through the yard. The jasmine plant caught my eye. I thought about picking a sprig for luck, but decided it wasn't worth the time. I sprinted across the grass and into the house, sped though the halls, and headed for the hidden staircase. I stopped in front of the doorway and turned on my pen-light. Shaking the hair out of my eyes, I started up the stairs toward the attic.

The door opened with a harsh squeak, like it didn't want to let me in. I looked around the cluttered room. It was too dark to tell if there were piles of my great-aunt's ashes littering the floor. I stepped over the boxes and around the menacing piles, wondering why I had been banned from the attic. Why did the rescued bird send me back here? Weak rays of light filtered through the dirty little window and I walked toward them. When I got to the far side of the attic, I saw it. Underneath a pile of dusty cardboard cartons there was a flat rectangular box. It looked almost like a briefcase. *With a lock on one side.* I tried to wiggle it free. An ugly bug with too many legs scuttled out and sped across the floor, desperate to find the safety of another shadow.

I shined my penlight on the lock and looked at it through my magnifying glass. There was a curling design etched into the metal. Opening my Porta-detective kit to get the key, I looked at the impression I'd taken on the wax square. An excited thrill passed through me. The designs matched! I fished out the key and slipped it into the lock. *It fit.* Deciding it would be safer to open the box in my bedroom, I stood up and headed for the hidden stairs.

The front door made a dull thump as it closed far below, and I heard Aunt Caroline's voice. I held the box in one hand and put the key into my pocket, taking shallow breaths. Flattening my body against the wall, my head whipped back and forth as I looked for a way to escape. There wasn't one. I was trapped in the attic.

There was no way I could walk down the stairs until they were gone. Squatting in front of the doorway, I put my ear to the door and listened for clues to tell me where my aunt and cousin were. Their voices got louder and then faded away when they walked down the hall to Gwendolyn's room. I decided to run for it and scrambled down the hidden staircase with the box tucked under my arm.

I peeked out the door and then hurried down the empty hallway. My fumbling fingers struggled to fit the key into my new lock as Aunt Caroline's voice grew louder. "Lie down and get some rest, and I'll bring you some juice," she told Gwendolyn just as I got my door open. Slipping into my bedroom, I locked the door behind me and breathed a sigh of relief.

After lighting the red candle, I sat in the alcove with

the box in my lap, and slowly turned the rusted key.

25
Evelyn's Ouija Board

The lid opened with a creak. Inside there was a game board decorated with numbers and letters. Symbols around the edges reminded me of the Wiccan ones Kat liked to doodle. There was also a heart-shaped triangle made of wood. Outside of that the box was empty. I read the printing that ran across the inside of the box: *Ouija Board*. "Why would someone bury the key to a Ouija board?" I wondered aloud. Aunt Caroline's words rang in my mind: *Stay out of the attic. Aunt Evelyn's things are up there*. It only took me a second to put two and two together.

It was Great-Aunt Evelyn's Ouija board. So *that's* who had planted the forgotten garden, and why it had been left to survive on its own. I couldn't wait to share the news with Kat, and pulled out my cell. I called her right away and spilled it. "The forgotten garden was my dead Great-Aunt Evelyn's. I saw the rescued bird outside my bedroom window. She stared at me, and then looked up at the attic like she wanted me to go back there."

"And that's where her feather pointed," Kat reminded me, as if I needed reminding.

"Exactly. I sneaked back up to the attic to look for the missing lock, and I found a flat box with metal lock on it. It has that same curling design as the buried key."

"And?" Kat asked impatiently.

"The key fit perfectly."

"What's in the box?" she demanded.

"Just a Ouija board and a wooden triangle." I'm sure she heard the disappointment in my voice.

"Ooh—that's excellent," Kat said, like she knew something I didn't.

"Why is that excellent?" I had hoped the old key would unlock something more exciting, like a treasure chest.

"Because," Kat explained slowly, "the Ouija board will tell us when it's the best time to plant the gems."

Saturday morning when I walked into the kitchen Aunt Caroline looked at me with fear in her eyes. "Skylar," she said, pausing while her fingers tapped the countertop, "Gwendolyn has mononucleosis. I hope you haven't already been exposed. It is contagious, so you should stay away from her. Most importantly don't share food, drink from her glass, or eat off her fork."

Ew. No problem there.

I nodded. Staying far away from Gwendolyn was fine with me. Then guilt punched me in the stomach. *Was it possible that Kat and I had actually given her mono with the incantation?* My cousin could definitely be a pain, but I hadn't wanted to make her deathly ill. "Where do you think she got mono?" All the energy flowed out of me as I waited for my aunt to answer. Sharing food wouldn't be an issue. I couldn't remember Gwendolyn ever offering me a bite of anything our whole lives. But the thought of making a family member sick didn't make me feel good at all.

"Several kids are sick with it. The doctor said it's going around."

I let out my breath. *Maybe it wasn't our fault after all.* "OK, I'll stay away from her," I promised.

Kat came over after lunch and I told her about Gwendolyn. "Mono?" she asked. "Awesome. The incantation worked."

I stared at Kat. *Was she actually happy that we might have made someone get really sick?* "My aunt said it's going around." *So it wasn't really our fault. Was it?*

"Still, she might not have caught it if we hadn't weakened her powers." Kat nodded at me with a superior look on her face.

I hoped my dad was right: that witchcraft was fake and there was no way we could have given Gwendolyn mono. But if our incantation had really caused her to get sick, there was much more to magic than I'd ever thought was possible. It made me question everything I believed about the supernatural. Maybe it wasn't all hocus pocus like my parents and Devon thought.

Even worse, was everything my parents taught me about reality all my life actually just—wrong? Could my dad, the genius chemist, actually not have a clue? How could I ever trust my parents' advice again?

And there wasn't anyone I could talk to about it. Alexa was away at summer camp and she was only allowed to use her phone in an emergency. I couldn't tell my aunt and uncle what we'd done. There was no way I was about to call Europe long distance and bother my parents with this. Kat would just roll her eyes at me if I told her how I was feeling. Maybe the Ouija board would spell out the answer I was looking for.

Hiding in the hallway at the top of the stairs, we waited until we heard my aunt talking on the telephone in her bedroom. Then we sneaked the Ouija board downstairs and took it with us into the garden. Kat sat down in the corner by a fluffy new patch of maroon and magenta nasturtiums. "Do you know how to use one of these?" I asked.

"Of course." I should have known. "Sit so you're facing me." Kat placed the Ouija board across our knees, setting the heart-shaped triangle on top of it. "Place your fingers very lightly on the edge of the pointer." We rested our fingertips lightly on the triangle, and almost instantly it began to move.

26
A Pathway Back into My Body

"You must be pushing it." I looked at the moving triangle in disbelief. The pointer zipped crazily around the board, carrying my fingers with it. It didn't stop on any of the numbers or letters.

"No, I am not. The psychic vibrations control the direction." The back of my neck prickled. I wasn't pushing it and it didn't feel like Kat was either. The heart-shaped triangle finally slowed and stopped. "Let's figure out what it wants to tell us. Empty your mind."

"Do the grounding?"

Kat looked at me. "Yes."

I pictured a long root flowing down my spine and into the dirt. Then I felt a golden glow connecting me to the earth. A warm feeling sped up my back and I was glad my spirit had a pathway back into my body. Kat and I looked into each other's eyes, and then the pointer started to move. Fast.

It sped across the board and landed on *E*. Then it veered to the other side and picked out the *V*. "Oh no," I said, as it sped back to *E* and over to *L*. Then it zoomed straight for the *I*. "Wait, this isn't how you spell—"

"Shh. Let it finish."

It landed on *N*. And stopped. "Either it tried to spell *Evelyn*..." I said.

Kat finished my thought. "Or *evil in*."

"Either way, it isn't a very good speller."

We looked worriedly at each other as the pointer

took off again. It chose *G* and then *A*, picking up speed. It landed on *R*, looped around and stopped on the *D*, bumped next door to the *E*, and carried our fingers over to the *N*. "You were right, Sky, this was your Great-Aunt Evelyn's garden," Kat whispered.

"Either that or it's trying to tell us there is *evil in* this garden."

"Maybe both."

"Wait—it's moving again."

It quickly spelled out a sharp warning: *NO MOR BAD SPELS*

"It thinks *we're* the evil in the garden!" I snatched my fingers off the pointer as if it was about to burn me. Kat stared into my eyes with the same shocked look on her face that I felt on mine. "Kat, it thinks we're doing black magic."

We watched the wooden triangle, half expecting it to move on its own. It stayed where it was, pointing to the *S*. Kat looked up. "The spell to weaken Gwendolyn's powers was the only dark one we can do. It obviously upset the vibrations in the garden. We have to concentrate on using our powers for good things. White magic only."

"Definitely," I said, nodding quickly.

"Should we see if it wants to tell us anything else?"

"OK," I agreed, slowly putting my fingers back on the pointer. I really didn't want to touch it again.

At first it didn't move at all. We thought the Ouija board was through communicating with us. Then the triangle started to travel. It sped smoothly across the board from letter to letter until it spelled out a whole sentence perfectly. As I read it, a shiver shot through my body. It started at the top of my head and went down my spine, through my root, and into the ground.

PLANT GEMS NOW.

27
Witch's Starter Kit

"There's no mistaking that message," Kat said excitedly. "It's time to plant the gems *now*."

A thrill shook me. Too many strange things were happening. They couldn't all be coincidences, could they? I didn't care if my dad thought witchcraft was baloney. *Maybe the gem seed spell could actually work.* "What do we use for seeds?"

"I'm not sure. We need to ask my sister." Walking quickly through the yard, Kat glanced toward the stables. She stuffed her hands into her pockets and looked at me sideways. "Is Carlos around today?"

I nodded. "Probably. Why?"

Kat looked away for a minute. Then she stared at me. It felt like a challenge. "I'm working on a love potion."

"For Carlos?" I laughed, and she gave me such a dirty look that the smile fell right off my face. "Sorry Kat, I just never thought of him that way."

"Good," she said smoothly. "Because you're going to help me figure out how to get him to drink it." Before I had a chance to object, she continued. "Why don't you ask your aunt if you can sleep over tonight. Wister is meeting at our house and there will be lots of people we can ask for advice about the gems."

I got quiet, trying to think up an excuse not to go. Kat looked at me funny and asked, "What's wrong? Does my family creep you out?"

I decided to tell a white lie. "No. Not at all."

My lie would come back to bite me, times ten. If I had any idea what was going to happen on the beach and the horror that would follow, there's no way on earth I would have agreed to sleep over.

Kat's parents had gone to a private screening of a friend's new movie and an after party, so they wouldn't be home until very late. They left us alone with a take-out menu and a wad of cash. "Wister usually meets at midnight," Kat said, helping herself to another slice of pizza. "But since my parents aren't here the other Wiccan goddesses are coming to our house tonight around ten. I got permission from Diana. We're going to witness their meeting."

"What-*ever*," Devon muttered, standing up. He brushed curly black hair out of his eyes with a delicate hand. "There's a full moon tonight, if you want to see it through my telescope," he offered me.

I was about to accept when Kat scraped her chair back. "Thanks anyway, but we'll be busy."

"Woo—ooo!" Devon moaned like a ghost, waving his hands in the air in front of Kat's face. "Busy doing a bunch of nothing," he muttered, running up the stairs to his bedroom.

I was munching on some salad, but suddenly I didn't feel hungry anymore. It was almost seven-thirty. "What do you want to do until ten?"

Kat didn't hesitate for one second. "Work on the love potion." Right then the beautiful strange music started, faint and far away. It sounded like it was floating down the hall from high above our heads, like the gloomy notes hovered close to the ceiling. From then on, whenever I heard haunting music it reminded me of the second scariest night of my entire life. The scariest night was still a few weeks away.

Kat led me back to her bedroom and walked over to the fire quadrant. She made a triangle from pieces of purple amethyst that she'd found in the hills, and set a fat red candle in the center. After lighting some rose-scented incense and the candle, she opened a black box.

"What's all that stuff?" I asked, peering inside. The shallow box was separated into tiny compartments. Some contained little red crystals or snips of herbs. Others held colorful stones and smelly items I couldn't identify.

"A witch's starter kit my sister made for me."

I pointed at a lumpy pile of maroon powder inside one compartment, wishing I had my notepad with me. "What's that?"

"Powdered raven's blood." She pushed curly hair out of her eyes.

"And that green goo?"

"You don't want to know. Put it this way, it came out of a frog."

"Gross."

"Uh-huh. I never use it."

"What about that gray ash? Was that something—" I was afraid to ask if whatever had burned up used to be alive.

Kat looked at me with one eyebrow raised. "It's not powdered rat, if that's what you're wondering. Witches burn their written spells after they write them in their *Book of Shadows* so a warlock from an opposing coven won't get ahold of them. Like if Demonia found one of Wister's spells they could use their own spell to hex them." Missing the doubtful look on my face, she opened Diana's *Book of Shadows* and flipped to the section on love potions. "This one doesn't sound too hard to make, but Carlos has to drink it naked, outside, during a full moon."

I laughed out loud, picturing it. "Good luck!"

"I better find a different one."

"Take your time." I was starting to get very nervous about joining Wister's meeting. Truthfully, I hoped the love potion would take so long to make that we would miss it completely. But Kat picked up her chalice and quickly measured ingredients, stirring them with the stone sword. When the potion was finished she poured it carefully into a thermos, held it up, and nodded at me with a confident smile.

"So do you have any pets?" I asked, trying to distract Kat. Hoping she'd forget all about the meeting.

"No. I wanted a black cat for a familiar, but my dumb brother's allergic."

"What's a familiar?" I looked at the clock. Almost ten.

"Oh God, Skylar, it's an animal that helps a witch be successful in her magic. Usually a cat but sometimes a dog or a toad."

"Ew."

"I know, right? That's why I wanted the cat. Come on. It's time."

I tried hard to think of an excuse not to go to the meeting, but my mind was a complete blank. We walked into the dark hallway and headed for a closet at the far end. The door opened with a harsh squeak, and I peered into the shadows. "What's in there?"

Kat held the red candle. Her tilting eyes looked eerie in its flickering glow. "Secret passageway. Follow me."

Like at my aunt's house, there was a hidden staircase behind the door, but this one went down instead of up. I pressed my hand against the cold stone, trying to keep my balance. Following Kat down dark, curving steps, I tried to concentrate on the feeble candlelight instead of my nerves. Our shadows wavered against the uneven walls. "What's at the end of the passageway?" I whispered.

"The room where the coven has their ceremonies," Kat answered. "We need to hurry. They may have started already, and we don't want to walk in during the middle. They're going to raise the dead tonight."

28
Meeting of the Coven

We stopped in front of a narrow door. The tarnished brass knocker reflected our candle's flame. Imagining thirteen witches burning me with an evil look for interrupting their ritual, suddenly my feet wouldn't move. My sneakers felt like they were glued to the floor. "I'm sorry," I stammered. "I—." I couldn't bring myself to admit that Detective Skylar was chicken.

Kat gave me a dirty look. "Don't be a baby," she said, rapping the knocker three times.

A scratchy croak answered her knock. "*Enter.*" Kat pushed the door open as if it were heavy. I followed her into a low-ceilinged room with my heart pounding.

It was too small to be a basement, but too big to be a bomb shelter, like at Grandpa's old house. *A dungeon?* Hundreds of candles glowed in holders that were bolted to the walls. There was a sickening smell in the air that I couldn't identify. I shuddered, thinking about how much green frog goo it would take to stink up a space this size.

The witch with the croaky voice had long hair that was thick and snarled. We followed her over to the twelve other members of Wister. They sat cross-legged on a huge sheet of black material with a silver pentacle sewn in the center. We knelt down on the scratchy fabric behind Kat's sister Diana. She wore a shimmering floor-length dress with long flowing sleeves, and a matching scarf covered her head.

The high priestess sat at the tip of the silver pentacle. Wrinkles crisscrossed her face, and a small, diamond-shaped piece of gold looked like it was implanted in her forehead. "By the power of the great goddess, who commands silence when secret mysteries are performed, aid me! Turn your vengeance and influence against mine enemies' houses." I recognized the croaky voice from the old woman who had answered Kat's knock.

Thirteen witches' voices rose to a frightening wail. Some of them drummed on the floor with their hands while others wailed or cried, "Yes!"

I cupped Kat's ear and whispered. "They're talking about Demonia, aren't they?"

She nodded. "Yes. That's their enemy."

While the coven chanted, I pictured Aunt Caroline staring out the window and twisting her hands, looking at Shadow Hills. *She knows there's a coven practicing black magic in the mountains behind her yard. She's got to know. It explains everything.*

The high priestess continued and the others swayed side to side. Kat grabbed my right hand and I kept my other in my lap, holding my breath, hoping the witch to my left would forget—

Too late.

A rough hand grabbed mine, pulling it into hers. Muttering a prayer, she leaned into me, rocking back and forth, forcing me to sway. It reminded me of being scared in church the time I went with Alexa when we were little. Like everyone around me believed in something I knew nothing about, and because I didn't, I would pay. Incense clouded the air, making it hard to breathe. The old witch continued.

"In this Sabbat, the veil between the living and the dead is lifted and we look for wisdom and guidance. We celebrate the Goddess while our enemies praise the Horned One."

"What's on her forehead?" I whispered as softly as I could.

Kat cupped her hand and whispered back. I felt her hot breath on my cheek and in my ear. "That's her Center of Power. Messages flow back and forth through it from her to the person she wants to communicate with. Usually someone from the other side."

I scratched my forehead. My fingers came away moist. "What other side?"

Kat eyed me through the gloom. "Someone dead."

Diana walked over to a low table covered in burning candles and incense. She opened a flat, leather box similar to Kat's starter kit. This one was bigger and had several rows of compartments. She picked out pinches of powders and some little red crystals and dropped them into a chalice that was crusted in jewels.

The old witch with the golden diamond in her forehead began to wail. Several others joined the chant. The sound was horrifying in the smoky shadows. Diana set the jeweled bowl on one point of the star and sat down next to the high priestess at the tip of the pentacle. A beautiful blonde goddess walked up to them, reaching inside the pocket of her dark cloak. She tossed a pinch of silver powder into the chalice.

I fingered my amulet and held my breath. The chalice exploded into a bowl of fire and the old witch screamed in glee. I started to scramble to my feet but Kat grabbed my arm in an iron grip.

Diana looked at the other twelve witches. "Would someone like to ask a question?" The members of the coven murmured at each other and shifted around on the black mat. Someone behind me mumbled a prayer in a foreign language. It sounded threatening.

The goddess with the shining blonde hair raised her hand and Diana nodded. "Is my father at peace?"

When the high priestess answered, I jumped with the chills.

"I am, my sweet," a man's deep voice boomed.

I snatched my arm out of Kat's grasp and ran for the dungeon door.

29
Treasure Map

I let myself into Kat's bedroom, shutting the door behind me just as the tears came. *How embarrassing.* Was I actually afraid of witches? How could I become a real detective if I couldn't even make it through a meeting of a coven? Was I really just a big baby?

Her bedroom was dark. The fish bowl in the water quadrant glowed a feeble blue. I couldn't hold it in any longer. Overcome with shame, I lay on Kat's bed and had the cry I had been holding back since my mom and dad dropped me off at Gwendolyn's. It felt good to finally let out all the loneliness and anger I'd been trying to hide.

Miserable memories ran through my mind: my parents waving and driving away as I stood on my aunt's porch watching their car pass through the security gate and disappear. They knew how I felt about my cousin. *Was I really stuck here for two whole months?* I remembered smelling Gwendolyn's hairball burn, and feeling so guilty when Aunt Caroline told me she had mono. And what if my aunt made me take horseback riding lessons? There was no way I was climbing up onto the back of one of those huge snorting animals.

I wanted to go home, but home was locked up and empty. I was painfully aware that I couldn't leave. My parents had abandoned me knowing I'd be miserable here. Knowing Gwendolyn would bully me. Why else would my mom have said, "I'm sorry," as she kissed me goodbye? I pictured my new friend Kat, rolling her eyes and yelling at me.

Then I felt a gentle hand touch my shoulder and rolled over with a gasp. Devon stood next to the bed, looking down at me with a sad expression on his face. "What's wrong?" he asked seriously. "When I stopped playing my sitar, I thought I heard somebody crying."

"You did," I said, wiping my cheeks. "I don't know what's wrong with me. I feel like a big baby, but I really miss my parents," I admitted. "They went to Europe without me and they haven't even called."

"Maybe their cell doesn't work there. My dad's never does when he travels." Devon looked away. "At least that's what he says."

"No, they've texted. And my aunt said they called once when I wasn't home. They're blaming the time difference," I grumbled, shoving Kat's pillow toward the wall. I didn't admit how many texts and emails I'd gotten, and that what I really wanted was to hear my mom's voice.

"They're coming back, aren't they?" His gentle eyes searched mine.

It was too embarrassing to keep looking at him, so I stared at the floor and nodded. "They're coming back," I said, dragging my fingers through my hair.

Devon sat down on the bed next to me and kept talking. Like he really needed someone to listen to him. "I get depressed sometimes too. I get picked on a lot at school 'cause I'm so short and skinny."

"Being skinny isn't so bad," I said, swiping away my tears. "Almost everyone in my gymnastics class is thin. It's healthy."

"Yeah but I bet the kids in your class don't call you Skinny Bones Jones." When he bent his head down I noticed how fragile his neck looked. Even his lips were thin, and his chin was tiny.

"No, but my cousin pointed at my chest once and asked me if I'm sure I'm a girl," I admitted, making him smile. "It's OK to be skinny."

He stuck his small fist out toward me, knuckles forward. I pressed mine gently against his. "OK, so you can call me S.B.J. for short," he said, and I smiled. Talking to him had cheered me up. "Want to see my telescope?"

"Sure," I said, following him down the hall to his room.

Devon walked up to his telescope and aimed it at the sky, fiddling with a dial and focusing. "Check it out. There's Orion," he said, standing aside. "See? You can see his belt with the three stars."

I peered into the telescope and looked at the stars lined up in the constellation. They were so bright I felt like I could reach out the window and touch one. "This is great," I said. But there was another spot I wanted to see. "Can I re-aim your scope?"

"Uh, sure," he said, fidgeting. "OK."

I swiveled his scope to the right and it stayed in focus. All I saw were more stars. Bright pinpoints of white light. Then I pointed the telescope a little lower. Hoping I could see Shadow Hills behind Gwendolyn's house, across the coast highway and a few blocks over. Devon's telescope was amazing, but the hills were jet black. I couldn't see a thing.

Suddenly a pocket of shadow seemed to wink, and

146

disappear. Then, through the end of the scope I saw something else. Shadowy figures moving around a ring of fire.

"Look," I said, moving away. I wanted to show Devon. I didn't want to be alone in this.

But Devon moved aside like he didn't want to look. Like he knew what he was about to see. He shook his head and took a step back. "That's Demonia," he said. He waited for me to react.

"Go on."

When Devon answered he spat out the words like he was on fast-forward. "Diana says they've been cursing the hills forever. She says they're evil. My sister's fighting them, but she thinks it isn't working."

I felt a chill wrap around my body. Demonia *was* real. "What are they doing?"

"Nothing good," he said, looking at the floor. "My sister says during the full moon they raise the Cone of Power."

"What does that mean?" I asked, staring out the dark window.

"They stand in a ring, hold hands, and focus on a point above the center of the circle. They imagine success for whatever—black magic trick they're trying to do. Their energy rises up and forms a cone." He sounded like he was reciting a memorized description that he'd heard many times before. "They dance, drum, chant, dance back-to-back, and then release the energy to complete the spell." Devon's hands hung by his sides, his thin fingers curling up. He looked at me like he was wondering if I believed him. "Diana told me," he said, like it was proof.

I swallowed. "What kind of spell?"

"Don't worry about it; it's all phony." He sounded like he was trying to convince himself as much as me. "Although sometimes when I'm watching? I've seen like a bluish cloud floating above their circle."

"What is it?" I whispered.

"I thought it was smoke, but Diana says it's their energy." Devon rolled his eyes and looked away. Then he riveted his gaze right back at me, like what I thought about this was very important.

I remembered holding my hands an inch apart, or being palm-to-palm with Kat, and the heat I felt. "I've felt that energy," I said. "I think it is real."

Devon looked surprised, and then his tiny chin quivered like his mouth was forming words he didn't want to say. "Well then someone has to stop them. But Diana says they're too powerful." He turned away from me like he didn't want to talk about it any longer.

"Thanks for showing me your scope," I said.

"Don't say what we talked about." Now he looked scared. Of what, I wasn't sure.

I held out my hand to pinky swear, but Devon had already turned back to the window and was gazing out, his thin fingers white against the sill.

30
The Third Cave

When I got back to Kat's room I paced from one quadrant to another, wondering when she would get back from the meeting. Her witch's starter kit sat on the hearth in her earth quadrant. The lid was closed, tempting me. I turned toward the door and listened to see if I could hear her coming. The hall was quiet, so I flipped the top open. There was a list printed on the inside of the lid:

These Gifts are the Traditional Powers of Witchcraft:

1. To Bring Success in Matters of Love
2. To Bless and Consecrate
3. To Speak with Those on the Other Side
4. To Know of Hidden Things
5. To Call Forth Spirits
6. To Know Secret Signs
7. To Possess the Knowledge of Changing Forms
8. To Possess the Knowledge of Divination
9. To Cure Disease
10. To Bring Forth Beauty
11. To Have Influence over Wild Beasts
12. To Know the Secrets of the Hands

Reading this made me feel a little better about Kat. Success in love and curing disease were good things. White magic, not black, right? Then again, we might have hexed Gwendolyn right into catching mono. That was definitely not white magic.

I looked at my right foot, remembering how I couldn't control its direction under the willow tree. Making clockwise circles until Kat's pointing finger changed my foot's direction. Her energy was too strong. She totally dominated me. And if I couldn't even control my own body, what else could Kat do to me?

Just as I thought this, she burst through the door to her bedroom. I could tell by her devilish grin that she wasn't mad at me for running out of the meeting. "Look what I got," she sang, dangling a folded piece of paper in front of my face.

"Did you talk to Diana about planting gems?" I asked, reaching for the paper. Kat put her hand behind her back and didn't give it to me.

"Sure did. First she warned us that if we try to conjure treasure, we might get more than we bargained for. She said we might be asking for trouble."

"Forget it then. Let's just plant pansies or roses."

Kat looked at me angrily. "You didn't let me finish. She said if we try to grow gems on something that is already alive, we might have problems since we are trying to alter nature." Kat slowly unfolded the paper, like she was trying to decide whether or not to share it. "Then she gave me this." She showed me the page. The crumpled paper was covered with circles, arrows, footprints, and symbols.

"A map?" I reached for it again, but she didn't hand it to me.

"Yes. This will show us where to find the seeds we

need to grow the gems. See this symbol? This is North, and here's the ocean," she said, pointing. Kat lit a blue candle in her water quadrant, put three sacred stones in her pocket, and handed me three. "We have to go to the beach, do the shell spell, and then look for three caves."

"First thing in the morning?" I asked hopefully. When she answered, I froze.

"No. At midnight. Tonight."

"Tonight? But it's—"

"What?" she interrupted. "Dark?" Kat looked at me like I'd just spit in her soup. She put one hand on her hip and arched an eyebrow. "You're not chicken, are you?"

I started to wish I'd never agreed to sleep over. "No," I lied. "But I'm not allowed—"

She interrupted me. "No one's going to catch us. They won't even know we went down there."

You're right, I thought. *My parents are a million miles away. And they couldn't care less about what I'm doing tonight. They aren't even thinking about me. Obviously.*

"Besides, the beach is really like my front yard. Just think of it like that. We're going to look for something we need that is in my front yard." Kat got that challenging look on her face again. Walking over to her water quadrant, she filled her pockets with shells, white pebbles, and some shiny pearls from her witch's starter kit. Then she pulled the petals off a drooping white rose, counted out nine, and threw the rest in the trash.

Even though I was afraid, following a treasure map and investigating caves sounded so adventurous that at the stroke of midnight I found myself following Kat outside. Creaky wooden stairs led down the rocky hillside behind her house to their private beach. The sea smelled like fresh fish and wet salt. Sliding my hand along the rough rail, I hoped that the worst thing that would happen to me tonight would be getting a splinter in my palm.

Silver-gray clouds slid past the moon, casting huge shadows on the sand. All too soon we reached the end of the staircase and I smelled the stench of dead mussels clinging to rocks. I paused with my fingers still touching the railing. As soon as I let go there would be no turning back. A cold breeze kissed my cheek as if to wish me luck. Or to warn me.

Violent waves slammed ocean water against the sand. Each pounding crash sounded like a car accident. Pausing with my shoe still touching the last stair, I wondered if there was any way to talk Kat out of this. She looked at the map, and then her legs powered across the sand and I knew it was hopeless. I figured that following her was better than getting lost on the beach in the dark, so I stumbled after her, scared to death. "Where are we going?" I asked, hugging my arms in the chilly air.

"To the caves on the beach," she said slowly, like she wanted to add, *Duh.* Kat plowed forward with determination in every step. Then she suddenly turned to her right and headed toward the raging waves. "But first, the shell spell, to ensure our success."

Kat walked toward the ocean and I followed, relieved when she stopped at the dark wet sand. The whitewater rushed toward us and we ran backward before it wet our shoes. Kat pulled a big shell out of her pocket and set what looked like a sunflower seed in the center. The clouds shifted and the moon appeared, lighting the sand around us. Standing behind Kat, I watched her kneel down and place the shell on the sand. She drew a triangle around it with her finger.

"What's that?" I asked.

"A symbol of our desire," she murmured, so softly it sounded like she was talking to herself. "So that the sea powers will receive the spell." I had to strain to hear her over the roaring of the waves. She looked up at me over her shoulder. "So we find the gem seeds?"

I nodded. To let her know I got it.

Then she pulled the pearls, white pebbles, and flower petals out of her pocket and set them down in a circle around the shell with the seed on it. "The tide has to bring the waves across the shell," she said, as the white-water sizzled forward, but not close enough. "And now the words of enchantment." Kat cleared her throat and began to speak slowly as the sea welled up in the distance.

"Goddesses of Moon, Earth, and Sea, my wish in thy names must come to be. Powers and forces which tides do make, I summon your waves, my spell to take." She stood up and we backed up into thick, dry sand just in time. A powerful wave broke, sending whitewater splashing across the wet sand and over the shell and back, carrying the seed and her other offerings out into the dark ocean.

Kat brushed sand off her hands. "OK, we're done here. Now, to the caves. We're looking for the third one."

I tried to keep my voice from shaking. "The third cave?" Another huge wave slammed the shore and I felt it vibrate beneath my feet. The water hissed and rumbled as it moved down the beach like a train escaping down a track.

"Yes," she called over her shoulder. "The map shows a series of caves, and we need to look inside the third one for the gem seeds. We just have to be careful that the tide doesn't come in while we're inside a cave. Or we'll get trapped."

She walked faster. I followed with my heart pounding, imagining cold water flooding into a cave and drowning us. I wished that I had brought my pepper spray—or a life jacket. Something that would protect me. From what, I wasn't sure. Looking back the way we'd come, I hoped to spot Kat's house up on its stilts so I knew how to get back. But the coastline had curved and I couldn't even see the staircase any longer.

"Sky," Kat cried suddenly, pointing across the black sand. "Look. There they are." I was more concerned about the rising tide, and looked out over the dark rumbling ocean. White spray flew up in the air as another huge wave crashed nearby. So loud it sounded like a refrigerator fell off a tall building and landed right next to us. I hurried after Kat as the water rushed forward. "This is it. Three caves." Moonlight cast shadows behind the boulders that guarded the entrance. We darted around them and climbed under the rock arch.

The dark cave stunk of washed-up kelp, dank and rotten. I shuffled forward on the damp sand with my hands out in front of me like a sleepwalker, hoping I wouldn't stumble over a rock or bash into a wall. I pulled out my flashlight and turned it on. As soon as its beam lit up the cave, heavy flies woke up, buzzing around the seaweed and bonking into my face. I ducked, swatting them away. Kat hurried past me and rushed toward the back of the cave, peering at the ground. Suddenly she cried, "Sky—here they are. I found the gem seeds!" Hidden between the boulders, disguised as wet pebbles, shining gem seeds winked up at us.

Bending down with my hands shaking and the flashlight beam bobbing, I picked up seedpods as fast as I could while the icy water crept closer and closer. I had a handful of pods when it became too late to stay another minute. A huge wave exploded on the beach and cold air poured into the cave. Seconds later seawater soaked through my tennis shoes, freezing my feet.

The tide was coming in. "Kat—we have to leave. Now!"

She looked outside the cave and the shock showed on her face. Whitewater covered the rocks and sand that separated us from the ocean. "You're right. If we stay here any longer we'll get trapped." Kat rushed past me and I hurried behind her out into the freezing air. I dropped a gem seed but I didn't care. Kat tore across the sand so fast I could barely keep up. If she lost me and another huge wave broke, I was dead. My feet churned through the wet sand and my calf muscles started to ache but I kept on running. It was so dark I wasn't sure we were even heading toward her house. I just followed the sound of her feet crunching the sand, gulping air as I ran, afraid I would suddenly feel someone's hand on the back of my neck or a freezing wave breaking over my head. It was so dark I couldn't tell if I was getting closer to Kat's house or if I was about to stumble into the sea.

Then I saw it. In the distance a tiny light flashed on and off, like it was trying to guide us home. My heart sped up. Kat and I ran toward it and it got brighter. I turned my flashlight on and off, signaling back. Strong waves smashed the shore as we plowed across the sand. It felt like we ran for blocks before finally reaching the back staircase. Devon stood at the bottom. The flashlight was so heavy it was straining his fragile wrist. He clicked it off for the last time.

"We made it," Kat said triumphantly, like it was her accomplishment. She shoved past her brother, heading up the wooden steps.

"Glad you did," he said, looking me in the eye as he dropped the heavy flashlight to his side.

"Thank you," I said, panting. "How did you know?"

"She always sneaks out at night," Devon whispered. "I figured she wouldn't wait for you and you might get lost." He held out a small fist to bump my knuckles and I grabbed him in a hug instead. Then I staggered up the creaky stairs behind Kat, holding the gem seeds tightly in my fist.

31
Evil in the Garden

The next morning we slept late, exhausted from the night before. When the sunlight filtering through her blinds warmed my face, my eyes cracked open. I woke up snug in my sleeping bag and looked around the unfamiliar room, surprised to find that I wasn't the first one awake. Kat stood next to the fishbowl in her water quadrant, bending over the gem seeds. When she heard me moving she whirled around with a guilty look on her face. She slipped her hand quickly into the pocket of her robe.

Did Kat just steal some of the gem seeds?

Struggling out of my sleeping bag, I joined her in the water quadrant and got my first look at the seedpods in the daylight. They were tan and smooth, shaped like shiny teardrops with pointy ends. I frowned. "You really think those things will grow into gem bushes?"

Kat looked at me like I was missing a few brain cells. "Of course they will grow into gem bushes. What do you think we went through all that for last night?"

"That doesn't necessarily mean—"

She interrupted, making a face at my morning breath. "You need to brush your teeth." Kat turned back to the seeds and arranged them in a circle. "Come on, Sky. Get your stuff together and let's get going."

"Where?" I actually felt like I could use a little break, and wanted to go back to my aunt's house by myself. Some time away from Kat sounded really good. And something about the three caves was bugging me. But I couldn't figure out exactly what it was.

"Don't you remember what the Ouija board said? It's time to plant gems. *Now*." She locked her witch's starter kit and stared at me, waiting for me to hurry up and get ready. I gathered up my belongings and threw them into my overnight case. Then I rolled up my sleeping bag while I kept one eye on Kat.

I went to the bathroom to brush my teeth and try to think of an excuse to leave without her. But the look in her eyes told me she was determined to come over and plant the gem seeds—today.

We walked downstairs, Kat carrying the seedpods that I'd wrapped carefully in a damp paper towel. If there was any chance they really would grow gems, we had to do whatever it took to keep them alive. I should have counted them the night before. Were some of the gem seeds missing, hidden away in the pocket of Kat's bathrobe? If only I had time to sneak back into her room and search it.

Kat's housekeeper gave us a ride back to Aunt Caroline's house, and I flicked the seatbelt buckle while I thought. As we drove down the coastline past the rumbling ocean, I suddenly realized what was bothering me about the caves. If Kat lived so close to them all along, why did she act surprised when we found the third cave? *"The beach is really like my front yard. Just think of it like that. We're going to look for something we need that is in my front yard."* She'd probably been playing in those caves all her life. There was no need for a map. Kat could even have hidden the gem seeds there for us to find. But why go to all that trouble?

After thanking Kat's housekeeper for the ride, we walked into Gwendolyn's house.

"It stinks in here," Kat muttered.

"I know," I said, distracted. *Should I question Kat about the caves? Or wait to catch her in a lie?*

I led her upstairs to my room and Kat locked the door behind us. "What do you want to do first?" she asked. "Give Carlos the love potion, or do the spell to grow the gems?" Kat took the thermos containing the love potion out of her backpack.

Gwendolyn's raspy breathing rattled down the hall-way. A pang of guilt poked me. "This is white magic, right?"

"Uh, *yeah*. Remember? 'NO MOR BAD SPELS,'" Kat said, drawing quotation marks in the air.

Grabbing my amulet, I put it around my neck. Fastening it slowly, I stalled for time while I thought about the spells we were going to cast. I was afraid of what we'd awaken in the forgotten garden if we tried to plant gems. Something weird was happening inside those overgrown walls. Could Evelyn's spirit actually be haunting Gwendolyn's house and grounds? Was the Ouija board right—was there evil in the garden?

I also felt guilty that Kat was trying to use witchcraft to attract Carlos. Was the love potion safe to drink? What did she really have inside that thermos? Was I about to poison the stable boy I'd known since we were kids? Picturing Kat's nasty reaction if I admitted my fears, I arranged a smile on my face. "Let's go plant gems."

We hurried down the stairs and ran outside, Kat carrying her witch's starter kit. Puffy white clouds with dark bellies hung low in the sky, dotting the garden floor with shadows. We looked around, trying to decide where to plant the seeds. Round nasturtium leaves jiggled in the wind. The pond water rippled and churned. I felt a chill, as if something had been released and flew through me, whisked up into the air on an invisible breeze. Kat looked at me with wide eyes, like she felt it too. Like something else was alive in the garden besides the plants and the two of us. I needed to move around and walked toward the roses.

"How about if we plant the gem seeds over here between the rose bushes and the pond?" I asked, kneeling down. "Here's a nice clear spot." I ran my hand over the smooth soil. An unexpected tingle vibrated against my fingertips. "I think this is definitely the right place." My voice sounded a lot calmer than I felt. "Kat, feel the earth right here," I whispered, looking over my shoulder into a shadowed corner. I had the crazy thought that there was someone inside the garden with us that I couldn't see. Kat sat down next to me and ran her fingers lightly over the earth like I had. She looked at me with her eyes widening. "Did you feel it too?" I asked.

She nodded her head with her hand hovering over the tingling soil. "You picked the perfect spot to plant the gems," she said, looking at me intensely. Then she opened her witch's starter kit and lit a green candle. "The vibrations are awesome. The earth is *asking us* to plant the gem seeds here." Kat pulled out the instructions that she'd copied from Diana's *Book of Shadows*, and read them out loud. "We need to make seven holes, seven inches apart.

We should have brought a ruler."

"I can measure that off, no problem," I said, poking the first hole in the dirt with my index finger. Bending that finger and holding it with my thumb, I pressed the space between my first two knuckles into the dirt seven times in a row. "That's seven inches." I poked a second hole and caught Kat staring at me. "The second part of my finger is an inch long." I held it up to show her.

Kat asked me the same question I had asked her about the witchcraft: "How do you know all this stuff?"

"From my detective work. You need to know how to measure things at crime scenes in case something happens when you don't have a measuring tape with you. Do you know how many inches long your feet are?" Kat shook her head. "You should find out." I finished measuring off the last seven inches and poked the final hole.

Kat unwrapped the gem seeds and read the instructions. "We'll plant one seed for each type of gem, and we drop a host of that gem's color into each hole at the exact same time as the seed."

"What's a host?"

"An object of the same color to represent the gem. Get it?" I nodded. "The gems have to grow in the order of the rainbow: red, orange, yellow, green, blue, indigo, violet. Imagine it, Sky," she said, searching my eyes, "a rainbow of gems—all ours. Picture seven bushes just dripping in jewels." She stretched her hand forward and waved it slowly across the area in front of us. Her eyes sparkled as she described our rainbow of riches. "Rubies, Agates, Topazes, Emeralds, Aquamarines, Sapphires, and Amethysts. We can sell them, Sky. We're going to be wealthy as queens."

This sounded pretty good to me. Excitement shot down my spine. Kat was starting to convince me that the spell could actually work.

She peered into her kit and pointed at little piles of colored powders, herbs, and tiny dried flowers. "We'll use powdered finch claw for the topaz, fresh Five Finger grass for the emeralds—it symbolizes power and wealth," Kat murmured. "You'll drop the gem seeds into the holes while I drop in a pinch of each host. They have to hit the bottom of the hole at the *exact same time*," she warned, "or the spell could fail." Kat pointed at the paper. She had written seven sentences in different colored inks. "We'll read each line together."

Then she pulled out a small jar and opened it. There was liquid inside. "What's—"

"Charmed water. I made it earlier," Kat told me. "Before you drop in each seed, dip it into the water. It will help them to sprout. Ready?"

She pinched up a bit of dried raven's blood, and I picked a gem seed off of the paper towel. I dipped the seed into the charmed water, and we held our hands over the first hole and read the first line. It was written in red. "By the power of Scorpio, Mars, and the raven, I name thee Ruby." When I dropped the seed, she released the pinch of dried blood into the hole at the exact same moment.

The seedpod hit the bottom. For a split second it glowed with a dull red light that came from the earth underneath it. The light disappeared instantly, mocking us.

"Did you see that?" I whispered, grabbing Kat's arm. *Did you* do *that?*

"Yes. I told you, the garden is *ready*. Pick up the second seed."

"By the power of Mother Earth, thunder, and the serpent, I name thee Agate." Dip. I dropped in another seed and she added a piece of lizard skin.

As soon as they reached the dirt, a tiny moaning sound floated up and out of the second hole. In moments, it disappeared as if it was never heard.

"Kat, this is scarier than the Ouija board." Goose pimples rose up on my arms. I wished my dad could see this. He wouldn't believe his eyes.

"It's not scary, Sky. It's *working*. Get another seed."

"By the power of sorcery, darkness, and the moon, I name thee Topaz," we chanted.

The gem seed plunked into the third hole with a pinch of powdered finch claw. A wisp of smoke curled up and around them, disappearing into the air. We stared at each other with our eyes wide open.

As I reached for another seed, a soft giggle escaped from behind the nasturtiums in the corner. I jerked my head around, looking for the laugher.

We were alone in the garden.

"Did you hear that?" I whispered.

"No," Kat said. I didn't believe her.

"You're sure your sister said this was safe?"

"Will you relax?" Kat hissed. "Grab another seed."

"By the power of Venus and Vishnu, I name thee Emerald."

A tiny cloud passed across the sun. A shadow hid

the fourth hole as a cold wind blew through my hair and chilled my arms. "Kat. Why aren't any of the leaves on the branches moving?" I asked her, barely moving my lips.

"They can't feel the wind," she explained gently. "It's meant just for us."

"By the power of fire, bewitchment, and the Evil Eye, I name thee Aquamarine."

As I pictured the gem seed blossoming into a blue jewel, a fiercely bright spark shot out of the fifth hole. It burned out in an instant.

"By the power of Neptune and Apollo, I name thee Sapphire."

I released the sixth seed. It hit the bottom of its hole and a sweet smell tickled my nostrils. Kat sniffed and looked at me. Then a subtle stench replaced the sweet, and her smile disappeared.

"You know what that smells like?" I asked, remembering a box of worms, grasshoppers, and beetles I had collected when I was ten. I'd forgotten that I'd hidden the box under my bed until the stench reminded me.

"What?" Kat looked almost as scared as I felt.

"It smells like dead bugs."

"I don't smell anything," Kat said. Now she looked confused. The smell had vanished.

I shook my head and tried to clear it. "I don't smell it now either. Let's finish this."

"By the power of prophecy and of the Violet Ray of Alchemy I name thee Amethyst." I let the seed roll off my fingers into the seventh hole. Kat released three dried violets, and suddenly the bottom of the hole began to shake and rumble.

"Look," Kat cried. We bent forward and watched the seed and the violets disappear in a fizzing, bubbling blur. The greedy earth seemed to suck down our offering like an elevator heading for the basement. I stared at the empty hole with my mouth open. Then the bubbles popped and the fizz cleared. The seed and the dried flowers rested in the bottom of the seventh hole, right where they should be.

I shivered and rubbed my hands down my arms, trying to get rid of the goose bumps. I hoped if Kat noticed she would just think I was cold.

"Now, as we blow the candle out and the smoke mingles with the air, so shall our spell become one with reality," Kat said. "Ready?" We blew out the candle and the smoke drifted around our heads. I pictured huge bushes brimming with buds, and the buds opening to reveal clusters of dazzling gems. We opened our eyes and Kat looked at me triumphantly. "Everyone at school will buy gems from us. They'll all want them, once we start wearing them. We're going to get rich." Kat gave me her superior look and nodded her head.

"How will they know that the gems aren't fake?"

Kat glared at me for a split second. "They'll believe you, Sky, if you tell them the gems are legit."

"Why would they?"

She looked at me like I had B.O. "You're one of those trustworthy people."

A bird streaked across the sky, shrieking a warning cry. I hoped it wasn't a crow. As we pushed earth into the seven holes and covered our seeds, I started to feel sick to my stomach. Like something had gone very wrong. We'd summoned something ugly.

A creepy tingle climbed up my neck. The evil in the garden was on its way back.

32
Love Potion

A breeze rustled through the forgotten garden. Flowers bent on their stems and dry leaves blew off bushes and settled in the corners. We walked through the gate, heading for the stable. "The gem seed spell was incredible," I said, wishing I had taken a video of everything we had seen. No one would believe it in a million years. Not that I was about to tell anyone.

Kat interrupted my thoughts. "It's totally going to work. I can feel it." She got that look in her eye that I was starting not to like. "Now for the second spell. Remember, you make Carlos run one of the horses, and when he's thirsty, I'll offer him something to drink." Kat held up the thermos containing the love potion.

"That stuff is safe to drink, right?" The inside of my nostrils felt dry and itchy. A brisk wind had started to blow.

"Uh, *yeah*. I like him, remember?" Kat shook her head as if I were stupid.

"*Hola*," I called, waving at Carlos.

He waved back. "*¿Que pasa?*"

I knew he would do what I asked, since my aunt and uncle were his bosses. "Exercise Lightning *por favor*," I said, pointing at the horse.

"OK, Skylar." Carlos mounted the white horse bareback, grabbing a handful of her mane. Kat gazed longingly at him as Lightning trotted away. Carlos's long, shining hair bounced off his tan back. Kat waited until she couldn't see him anymore before turning back to me. "Hey, how come you don't ride horses if your cousin always had them?"

How could I explain? "Um, I don't know, they always just seemed kind of—tall."

Kat tipped her head back and laughed at me. "You *are* afraid of horses! I thought so. Oh, that's too funny."

I felt my face turn red. "No I'm not." Looking down, I kicked the dirt with my foot.

"Yeah, right," Kat said under her breath, embarrassing me with my lie. "OK, prove it." Kat looked at me like this challenge was the ultimate test of our whole friendship. It didn't mean a thing that I'd followed her to the caves at midnight when I wasn't allowed. Or that I'd chosen Kat for a partner over Andy, when it was so important to him. That I'd hexed my own cousin, trying to keep her away from us. All of a sudden none of that mattered.

Exactly all that mattered was that I got on a horse. To prove to Kat that I wasn't chicken. Or that I would do whatever she told me to do.

Lightning cantered back toward the stable. Carlos's dark skin reflected the spotty sunshine. "Whoa," he said, stopping his horse right in front of us.

Kat seemed to know precisely what she wanted me to prove. Her knowing smirk said it all: Obey me. Face your fears. Don't be a wuss. I challenge you. Don't be a loser. Belly up. Do this. "Skylar wants to ride," she said, pointing at me and then at the horse, in case Carlos didn't understand.

"*No problema,*" he said, looking at me strangely. Carlos had never seen me get on a horse in all the years he'd worked for my aunt.

Kat turned to me and grinned. "You aren't afraid of horses, right?"

"No." I bent over and scratched my knee, hoping like crazy that Carlos was too busy to saddle up a horse for me.

No such luck. He disappeared inside the stable and came out five minutes later leading Brownie by her reins. I tried to breathe while I watched her feet clomp across the dusty ground toward me. I watched those heavy hooves kick up puffs of dirt. Looked at her spindly legs and the giant body that seemed too big for them to hold. Imagined climbing up on that broad back and broke out in a sweat.

Carlos noticed. "You sure? *Es* OK?" he asked, looking at me with concern on his face.

Feeling like I couldn't get enough air into my lungs, I reached up and patted Brownie's side. My grandfather's words echoed in my brain. *"The only way to conquer your fears is to face them head-on."* He wasn't talking about horses then, but I decided to take his advice and get over it. Right now, once and for all. I was sick of being a chicken. Sick of being embarrassed and ashamed. It was just a horse. *Just a big, giant, snorting, stomping animal.*

Pushing sweaty hair out of my face, I looked across the canyon, thinking, *I could do this.* I would do this. It was time to prove something to myself. I nodded. "I'm sure."

Carlos held out a stirrup and motioned for me to put my foot into it. Feeling like I could throw up at any second, I jammed the toe of my pink sneaker into the stirrup and took a deep breath. Kat elbowed Carlos and pointed at me, pretending that she was trying not to laugh.

I bounced one, two, three, and flung my other leg over the horse's back, the way I'd watched Carlos and my aunt do it dozens of times. All of a sudden, *I was up there.* I was actually on top of that big, beautiful beast. Across my cousin's yard and way past it I could see the ocean shimmering in the distance. Looking down at Kat, even though my heart was pounding, I smiled.

Now that I was ready to go horseback riding with Carlos, Kat's challenging grin turned into a frown. "Don't be long," she warned, folding her arms across her chest.

Brownie shifted side to side and pawed the dirt impatiently. *Did she not like having me on her back?* Hugging the horse's body with my thighs and holding tightly to the reins, I so wished I were anywhere else. Brownie stomped the ground and it felt like an earthquake. I didn't know which way she would move next. Whether I could balance or not felt like it was up to someone else. Alexa's text sprung into my brain: Dt wrry u wnt fal f. Oh how I hoped she was right.

Carlos swung himself up onto Lightning and made a *click, click* sound with his mouth. All of a sudden both horses started to trot toward the hills.

"Wait a minute," I called. "I'm not allowed—" but he couldn't hear me over the wind and their clomping hooves. Brownie strained forward, following Lightning toward a rough dirt path. Why wasn't I allowed to go into Shadow Hills, when Carlos obviously took the horses up there all the time? *If it isn't too dangerous for him, it isn't too dangerous for me.*

I was finally going to see what really went on up there.

The thought excited me enough that I forgot that I was sitting way up on the back of a gigantic animal. For about a second. Carlos stopped his horse and turned around to check on me. "It's OK," I said. "Let's go." I held the reins tightly and Brownie started to move. First she just walked, but then she sped up into a trot. The air whooshed past my face. I bounced up and down, my butt hitting the saddle over and over, jarring me until my teeth clacked together.

Carlos looked at me over his shoulder and pointed to his leg. "Hold hard to the horse," he called. As soon as I squeezed Brownie's body with my thighs, Carlos made that clicking noise again and the horses sped up into what my aunt called "cantering." Suddenly we were going fast. I wasn't bouncing up and down anymore. It was like my body became one with Brownie's, gliding smoothly forward as she cantered up the hill. We hit a straight path and my hair flew out behind me as Brownie surged forward. I was getting the hang of it. I was actually horseback riding. And I liked it.

Then the dirt path narrowed and became tighter and steeper. Brownie stopped cantering, then trotted, then walked. We were way past the pines now. Kat and Gwendolyn were far behind. So was everything familiar and safe. The striped rock that I'd seen from the windows of my parents' car was all around me now, sheeting toward the sky. No footholds anywhere. Climbing it would be impossible. This was dangerous turf.

I was halfway up into Shadow Hills.

Watching Brownie's hooves hobbling up the skinny

path, my old fear came gushing back. I felt like I was about to choke, watching her feet, so close to the edge of the cliff. Her hoof kicked a rock and it bounced down the side of the mountain: *plink...plink...tink*. If she slipped and we rolled down the hill I'd be dead in seconds. Brownie started to breathe hard, huffing as she panted up the trail behind Lightning. We rounded a bend, and the path widened.

The extra shadows Kat told me about started to appear. The sun disappeared behind a cloud. I thought I saw caves, and then I didn't. Brownie's hooves clip-clopped past dark patches of rock that became indentations as we passed them. When I looked over my shoulder, they disappeared. Was the sunlight playing tricks on me? Or was Demonia?

No time to worry about the shadows. We'd climbed so far up into the mountains that far below us Gwendolyn's backyard looked like a small patch of tan, a tiny blue pool, and a lot of trees. The sun started to set. There wasn't much daylight left.

Leading me into a clearing, Carlos stopped his horse and looked around. We'd reached the middle of the mountainside, where I'd seen the flickering lights. The part of the hills with extra shadows. I wasn't sure what I was about to find, but I had a queasy feeling it was going to be big. And that it would introduce me to something from which I couldn't climb back.

"Skylar," Carlos said, pointing to the ground.

I looked down and stared. A black circle was burned into the earth. Gray ashes fluttered here and there. Brownie stomped her hooves like she was impatient to leave. I leaned forward for a better look. A pile of bones rested in the center of the blackened circle.

"*Brujas. No bueno. ¿Comprende?*" he asked, and I nodded.

I didn't need to speak a lot of Spanish to understand. *Witches. No good.* It was all right here in front of me, plain as day. A ring of fire burned into the ground with a pile of bones in the center. A burnt offering. Something used to be alive, and now it wasn't. Something that had once been able to scream had been sacrificed.

Black magic.

I pulled out my phone and took a picture of the dark circle singed into the earth and the burnt bones in its center. Then I tossed my cell to Carlos. He caught the phone and stared at it for a second before figuring out how to use it. I held Brownie's reins up and tried to smile. Carlos aimed the phone, pushed a button, and nodded his head.

We had to go. Carlos tossed my cell back to me. He clicked his tongue at the horses, and off we went. Riding down the hill was even scarier than coming up. Puffs of dirt rose from around Lightning's hooves, making Brownie snort and shake her head. At any moment her foot could slip and we'd plunge down the hillside. My luck the horse would land on top of me. I felt like I was about to throw up. And it wasn't just from the horseback riding.

I remembered everything I'd just seen. Bones inside a ring of fire. Kat's words rang in my mind. "*During the full moon they have ceremonies. With sacrifices. You don't want to be anywhere near them when that happens.*" I followed Carlos down the path, swallowing saliva, praying I wouldn't barf.

Staring at the ground was making me dizzy, so I looked up and across the canyon at the ocean. The setting sun shimmered on the water, and small, glittering waves surged toward the shore. Wet sand reminded me of three caves and gem seeds, and the burnt bones I'd just left behind. I realized there were scarier things than horses, and that I'd finally ridden one. I stroked Brownie's neck, proud of myself for facing at least one of my fears. We rode back into Gwendolyn's yard and up to the stable. When we got closer to Kat she looked madder than I'd ever seen her. "What took you so long?" she demanded.

"You wanted me to go for a ride, right? So I took you up on your challenge." I held Carlos's hand as he helped me down off the horse. After I jumped to the ground, he wiped his shining forehead with a bandana. Kat glared at me, but she put a smile on her face as soon as Carlos looked at her. "I found some evidence," I said softly, so Carlos wouldn't hear me.

"Of what?" she whispered back.

"Demonia, I think. A ring of fire, singed into the earth. And some burned bones." I pulled the picture up on my cell and handed my phone to Kat.

She glanced at it and gave me a knowing look, like the slow child had finally caught up to the rest of the class.

33
Shape-Shifting Flowers into Gems

We walked the horses back to the stable and Carlos took them inside. When he came back, Kat pulled out the thermos. "You look thirsty," she said, offering it to him.

I froze, wondering what she really had in there.

Carlos nodded. "*Si*," he said, taking the thermos.

While Carlos swallowed the potion, Kat turned away and whispered the love spell. "Drink the potion, show the sign, swallow all, thine love be mine." I felt my fingernails dig into my palms.

"*Gracias*," he said, handing her the empty flask.

Kat nodded slyly and then we made our way back to the house. "Now we just have to hope it works." When I didn't answer right away, she looked at me defiantly. "Right Skylar?" she asked loudly.

I nodded, realizing that I really couldn't wait for her to go home.

The next few days passed without any drama. Every morning, thick fog edged across the ocean while I rode my bike or took the bus to school. Kat and I made our projects like we hadn't planted gem seeds or tried to grow a plant that would make us rich as princesses. We were just two regular kids, going to summer school and taking art. Shadow Hills was quiet at night, and the ring of fire started to feel like a distant memory.

"Hey Rudy," I said Thursday as I climbed onto the bus.

When I sat down next to him he opened his sketchpad and showed me his latest fairy-gnome war. Light blue-pink fairies dove down and attacked hunched gnomes in muddy brown hats. A wizard perched in the top right corner, looking down at the fighters. "That's awesome." Rudy tucked his bony elbows into his sides and thanked me by smiling bashfully. After the bus ground to a stop, we walked into class together. I signed *hi* to Andy and said, "See you later," to Rudy.

Kat sat down at our table and gave me a look. "Why are you talking to Rudy Beanpole?"

Like my choice of friends was any of her business. "What do you mean? Why wouldn't I?"

"He's a dork," Kat said.

"No he's not." I felt my cheeks grow hot, remembering how nice he was to me on the bus on the first day of school. How he'd stood up to Gwendolyn, and how she backed right down as he stood by my side.

"You shouldn't hang with him," she insisted.

"Why, because he's tall and shy?" Then I had a more disturbing thought. "Or because he's black?"

Kat shrugged. She looked at me and shook her head like I didn't have a clue.

"Whatever. He's a great artist," I said. "And I like him." As far as I was concerned, the conversation was over.

Later that afternoon, the fog lifted. White sky faded to blue, and the chill turned to balmy dampness. I started to feel normal again. Like I hadn't done anything wrong, had never cast an incantation under the willows. Gwendolyn was getting better and nothing bad happened to

Carlos. The love potion wasn't poisonous after all. Everything was fine.

But Friday after summer school I knew everything wasn't fine. Even though being friends with Kat had started to feel like wearing a fur coat in summer, I realized suddenly that I needed her more than ever. Standing in the forgotten garden I took out my cell, dialing her number as fast as I could. "*Kat. You need to come over. Right now.*"

"Did some of the seeds sprout already?"

"One of them did. It doesn't look like any kind of normal plant I've ever seen."

"It shouldn't. Maybe the spell worked and it's a gem plant." I heard the excitement in her voice. "Which hole?"

"It's not coming out of any of the seven holes exactly, but it's close."

"To which one?"

"Sapphire."

"Excellent. I'm on my way."

Kat ran through the gate into what she now called the Remembered Garden. I had watered every day with the hose, and thorny vines were blooming with thousands of crimson petals. Shocking magenta and orange flowers surrounded the pond. Wildflowers crept across the ground, blossoming in a frenzy of color. The skinny bush in the corner was covered in purple blooms.

"Look at this." I bent down in front of the patch of earth where we had planted the gem seeds. A funky golden spike had pushed its way out of the earth about an inch behind the sixth hole and curved crookedly toward the sky. None of the other seedpods had sprouted yet. "It looks kind of creepy. Do you think that thing will really grow sapphires?" I asked.

Kat looked annoyed when she saw the doubt on my face. "Diana's *Book of Shadows* said so." Then she shrugged as if it didn't matter what I thought. "Hopefully the next one will grow rubies. They'll be easier to sell." She peered down at the twisted shoot. "We'll know when we know. We just have to wait and see."

We didn't have to wait long.

Three days later the stalk was four inches tall. Juicy tan leaves sprouted out of each side and a greasy-looking bulb grew on the tip of the plant. The vine had started to bend down toward the ground as if its head were too heavy. I sniffed the gem plant. It smelled like skunk.

By Saturday the bulb had almost doubled in size. Lighting green candles all around the stem, we recited a growing spell. Kat tossed peppermint leaves and pinches of powder from her witch's starter kit onto the garden floor. We threw in some powdered bee balm to aid our success, and added three Yarrow leaves to make our spell more powerful. When we blew out the candles, I imagined a bud opening and a giant sapphire sparkling inside. I wondered what we would do if our spell actually made us rich. How would I feel if I found out that my parents had been wrong all along? Would they be proud of their daring daughter and of everything I had accomplished? Could my dad actually admit that sometimes there just wasn't a logical explanation?

More importantly, was this really white magic if I was

178

shape-shifting flowers into gems to make myself rich?

Monday after school Kat and I ran into the garden. The plant was taller and the bulb was larger, but the first leaves had rotted and fallen off. Kat knelt in front of it and gently lifted the pod with her fingers, like she was trying to weigh it. I peered at it through my magnifying glass. It just looked like an ugly tan balloon. "Is it heavy?" I asked.

"Not really. But there might be something inside it. Let me see that magnifying glass."

I laughed on the inside, but not on the outside. "It's just a mag glass. It won't help you see what's inside the bulb. We'll just have to wait until it's ready to open," I said. "Besides, if there is a gem in there, maybe it will get bigger if we give it time to grow."

Kat looked at me and nodded. "Excellent."

She came over on Saturday and we raced each other to the garden. Kat pushed past me to get through the gate and we ran up to the gem seed plant.

"Oh God, gross!" she yelled.

I gasped and scrabbled backward to get away from it.

The slimy vine had gotten taller and then wilted onto the garden floor. Black spots of mold decorated the thick stalk, and tiny wet leaves had started to bud where the first ones had fallen off. The bulb was larger and had split open along its seam. Beige worms tumbled across each other, writhing and wriggling to get out of the rotting pod. The smell was horrible. I put my arm over my nose and mouth, trying to breathe through my sleeve.

"Kat, we have to dig up the other seeds," I groaned.

"Something went wrong with the spell, I know it."

"What are you talking about?" Kat asked, glaring at me. "We have to give the other seeds a chance and see—"

I cut her off. "And see what other horrors we can grow in here? Maybe a dead-finger plant? Maybe a bush with deformed cat heads blooming on it?" I knew I sounded frantic but I didn't care.

"You're being ridiculous," Kat said, but she didn't sound convinced.

"You smelled death too, I know it. You saw the signs. This is what the Ouija board warned us about: NO MOR BAD SPELS. Well this was a *bad* one, Kat. Black magic. And we have to undo it." I pawed at the dirt with my hands. All of a sudden a horrible odor filled our nostrils. A lonely wind iced our cheeks in the still garden.

Kat's face sagged. "I think you're right," she agreed, digging into the earth. "This *is* the evil in the garden. Hurry!" She dug up the glowing-red ruby seed and tossed it behind her.

"What do we do with the other seeds?" I cried. "We can't leave them in here. It's supposed to rain. What if they replant themselves?" I dug up the emerald seed. It had a fat cutworm wrapped around it. I threw it onto the pile behind us.

"I'll take them down to the coven room and burn them," Kat offered, her voice gravelly. "Here's another one." She plucked out the Agate seed. It was covered in slime. "Ugh!" She flicked it off her finger toward the others.

When we had the six unsprouted seeds in a smelly, gooey pile, Kat dug up Evelyn's buried box. "Mind if I carry them home in this?"

"No. Just get them out of here," I said, wrapping a strand of hair behind my ear.

Kat looked at me with begging eyes. "Will you come over?"

I wasn't the only one afraid this time.

34
My Friend the Liar

"Well that didn't work," Kat said nastily, thrusting the *Book of Shadows* at her sister.

Diana laughed, resting a hand on her bony hip. "So, you planted the seeds without waiting for the new moon, didn't you?" she asked, one long black eyebrow cocked. "Couldn't wait to get rich, could you little sister? Trying to sidestep the rules of Wicca and take shortcuts? You're lucky all you grew were maggots." She spun around and marched out of Kat's bedroom, her silk cape flapping behind her.

Kat's dishonesty knocked the wind out of me. My temper started to boil. "You told me this was safe," I shouted. "You lied to me!"

My detective fantasy took over:

I unhooked a pair of handcuffs from my belt and slapped them around Kat's wrists, closing them tightly. "Get her out of my sight," I told the warden. "She needs to spend a week in solitary confinement. That will teach her not to lie to her friends and put them in danger." Kat hung her head in shame as a guard led her toward an empty cell.

"No I didn't," Kat said, gritting her teeth and looking at the floor. "I misunderstood the directions, that's all." She couldn't look me in the eye. That was a sure sign of a lie, but I decided to drop it. We had a more important problem. The gem seeds were still alive.

I stared at her with my arms folded. "How are you going to destroy the seeds?"

"I'll ask Diana if she'll get rid of them for us. Maybe she can say a blessing first and undo whatever we've done."

"Good idea. I wish I'd never seen those stupid seeds."

Kat stepped into her earth quadrant. She lit orange and green candles and a stick of sandalwood incense. Then she slumped down onto the floor, pulling little pots of growing things around her in a comforting circle. "I feel sick," she mumbled. "I can't believe we grew maggots. The garden spirits must be furious with us."

Kat's pouting made me even angrier. "We used a stupid bunch of seaweed pods that we found in a cave where we never should have been at midnight. Of course we grew something gross and slimy. It was probably our punishment for breaking the rules and sneaking down there." She glared at me and didn't say anything, so I continued. "Plus, that thing didn't exactly grow out of one of the seven holes. It could have come from some weird seed that was in that area in the first place. We watered and fertilized it, so it grew. And then it died, and flies landed on it, and they bred. Producing maggots. So it wasn't a maggot plant we grew from a sapphire seed, was it?" I flicked my thumb over and over across the piping on her bedspread. I wasn't getting a reaction so I talked a little louder. "Don't you think I'm right, Kat?"

"We just did the gem seed spell wrong," she insisted. Kat looked at me sideways and smiled crookedly. "We're going to have to try it again." When I didn't agree, her expression turned mean. "Right Skylar?"

"Whatever. I better get going." Glancing into her water quadrant, I noticed a thin layer of dust covered her fishbowl. The brown candle in the earth quadrant had started to melt in front of the sunny window and was slumping sideways. Kat's room didn't look as inviting in the fading afternoon light. I wiped the slime out of Evelyn's box with a fistful of Kleenex. Then I put the box in my backpack and headed for my bike, looking forward to getting away from my new friend.

When I woke up Sunday morning I heard rain drumming on the roof. The light coming through my window was dull and gloomy. A seagull floated on the air right outside, so still that he seemed to be flying sideways. I snuggled into my warm covers and enjoyed the cozy sound of the raindrops. An envelope covered with brightly colored stamps rested on my bedside stand. I picked it up and read the long letter from my parents for the fourth time.

It started with an apology.

Dear Skylar,

We miss you very much and are so sorry we haven't been able to talk to you. The tours have kept us on the go non-stop, and with the eight-hour time difference it just hasn't been very convenient to call. Your father and I cherish every one of your texts, and really wish you were here. We know you are a strong and independent girl, and are probably having a fabulous time (we hope) without us.

They talked about how beautiful Europe was, but said the World War 2 monuments would have been even more interesting and the French food would have tasted so much better if I had been there to enjoy it with them. They told me that they were thinking about me all the time, and reminded me that it would only be a few short weeks until we would all be home again. Seeing my mom's handwriting and hearing that my parents missed me made my whole chest fill up with happiness. I couldn't wait until they picked me up and we were driving down Pacific Coast Highway, heading for home.

My very own bedroom and my bigger, more comfortable bed were waiting for me. I was looking forward to decorating four quadrants with plants, candles, and bowls full of colored water, glitter, and seashells. There hadn't been any time for creative writing since I met Kat. I missed my big old desk with its secret compartments where I hid money, and its drawers full of blank paper waiting to be filled with stories. I wouldn't hear drumming or chanting from behind my bedroom window, and there weren't any covens doing witchcraft in the hills behind my house.

I thought of my BFF, Alexa. It had been weeks since she'd left for camp and we could talk or text. I remembered all of our silly private jokes. We could laugh our heads off for hours, cracking each other up with comments about ourselves and the funny things that happened to us. When I thought about Kat laughing at the other people in Miss Yamato's class, I realized there are very different types of funny.

Late that afternoon the sky finally cleared, and I walked across the muddy path toward the garden. Kneeling down in front of the wicked vine, I was relieved to find the stem twisted and flat, and the maggots dead and gone. The dirt that covered the other six holes hadn't moved. The garden no longer stunk of rot. Sitting down in front of the old fountain, I stared into the rainwater that had collected inside what Kat and I called *the chalice*. Now it just looked like an old, crumbling fountain. I wondered if Great-Aunt Evelyn had sat here and looked into it, thinking about things when she had been alive.

Then I glanced up at the small window above my bedroom. It was dark, and nothing moved behind the glass. The rescued bird soared from the twisted oak tree to one of the willows where she was building a nest. As the shadows lengthened, I thought about something that made the back of my neck tingle.

I remembered a birthday party I'd had when I turned six. My dad hired a magician to perform for my friends and me. We'd giggled at the live bunnies and were amazed by his card tricks. He made coins disappear, and then they'd reappear inside our pockets or he'd pull them from behind our ears. Once we all turned around to hear someone invisible call out from behind the fire-pit. After his last magic trick, the magician pointed dramatically at my shoe. A tiny explosion went off right next to my foot, and it scared me so much that I cried. The magician felt so bad that after the party ended he showed me how he did the trick: He threw a little object called a TNT popper at the ground which exploded on contact, making a loud bang and a little puff of smoke.

"Did Kat create everything that happened in the garden to impress me?" I wondered aloud as my stomach sank. *Was the gem seed spell just a giant magic trick?*

Moving into the corner of the garden, I peeked under the big nasturtium leaves looking for blossoms. Bumpy green seeds grew where flowers had died and fallen off.

Older seeds had turned tan, dried up, and shriveled like raisins. Poking little holes in the soil near the area where we had planted the evil gem seeds, I popped in the tan nasturtium seeds, wondering what would grow.

35
A Piercing Scream

Wednesday after school Carlos helped me up onto Brownie's back again. This time we stayed out of Shadow Hills. He'd shown me what he wanted me to see. Kat was right about one thing: An evil coven was practicing black magic near Gwendolyn's house. There was no way was I going back into Demonia's territory.

Brownie followed Lightning onto the horse track and soon we were cantering around the circle. My neck cooled as my hair flew up and out while I glided around and around. It was like a ride at Magic Mountain, but better. The best thing I ever did was to quit making excuses and just do it. By Saturday Carlos had me galloping. Aunt Caroline watched me, tapping the kitchen windowsill with a big smile on her face. It wouldn't last long.

When we finished our ride, Carlos helped me off Brownie's back and motioned for me to wait while he stabled the horses. He came out of the barn and curled his finger: *Follow me.* Carlos was frowning. Like whatever he was about to show me wasn't going to be good. We walked over to Gwendolyn's goat pen and he pointed at the ground by the gate. A black sack that was slightly bigger than a deck of cards rested in the dirt. I picked it up and looked inside. The bag contained a sewing needle, a twig, a coin, and a thimble. *A sewing kit?* "What is this?" I asked Carlos.

"*Preguntar a su amiga,*" he answered. *Ask your friend.*

He shook his head, leaving me alone with the bag in my hands. The little black goat, Shena, hobbled over to the fence and stared up at me. Her brown eyes looked soulful and expectant.

"Sorry, Little One, I don't have any treats," I told her. She cocked her head and showed me her teeth as if she were smiling, letting me know it was OK. I reached my hand over the fence and pet her between the ears. She didn't bite me. In fact, I think she liked it. When she trotted away her stubby tail was high in the air.

I crossed the yard and clomped up the stairs to my room, fingering the black fabric, wondering who dropped the sack. When I got to the alcove seat I called Kat. She answered right away like she was expecting me to call.

"I found a weird little bag outside the goat pen," I said softly, in case Gwendolyn was eavesdropping.

"What is it?"

"A small black sack. Want me to email you a picture of it?"

"What was inside it?"

"A needle, a thimble, a twig and a—"

Kat interrupted me before I could finish. "And a coin?"

The back of my neck prickled. "How did you know?"

"This is bad. That's a Nanta bag. Those items? They're miniature ritual tools. The coin is the pentacle, the twig is the wand, the needle is the athame, and the thimble is the chalice."

"Did you drop it?" I asked, knowing the answer.

"Sky," she said, like I was that slow kid again. "Wake up." Kat exhaled into the phone. "Someone from Demonia was in your backyard."

On Monday Kat and I ran upstairs to my room after school, hurrying so we wouldn't run into Gwendolyn. I didn't want her to threaten to ruin my new art project before I could put it away. We'd made dream catchers and mine turned out really good. I also didn't feel like explaining that witches from an evil coven had been sniffing around her goat pen. Not that there was anything I could do about it. Whether or not she was still contagious, it was better to just avoid my cousin completely.

I put the dream catcher away in my art supplies drawer. After weaving aqua and sea-green colored yarn back and forth across a wire circle, I'd glued little seashells between the knots on the frame. I planned to hang it up between my air and water quadrants as soon as I got back home and redid my bedroom. Dream catchers were designed by Native Americans to prevent bad dreams. I wished I had something that would prevent bad luck, because I had a feeling some might have just headed my way.

My cousin started banging away at the piano downstairs, practicing her latest lesson. "Gwendolyn's busy," I said to Kat. "That's good. She won't follow us." I locked my door and we headed for the garden. "I found all these nasturtium seeds," I said, "and planted them near where the maggot plant grew. I thought maybe the soil would still have some fertilizer in it from all the stuff from your starter kit. I want a pretty plant to grow there, so I don't have to think about—"

Kat shuddered. "I know. That was horrible."

"I planted them right over here. Look," I cried, kneeling down. One seed had already started to push firmly out of the ground. Its tender white stem bent like the graceful neck of a swan with its head stuck in the soil. "Most of them aren't all the way out yet." There were lots of tiny white nubs, and I knew in a few days I'd have plenty of little seedlings. *Hopefully they aren't Evilroot*, I thought.

"Maybe they need a drink," Kat suggested, so I brought the hose over. "Don't turn it on very hard; you don't want to drown them."

"No kidding," I said, turning it on to barely a dribble.

After I moistened the soil around the nasturtium sprouts, Kat mumbled a feverish incantation. "Are those green candles still back here?" she asked.

"One is. I hid it in Evelyn's box." Pushing a pile of dead weeds aside, I opened the wooden box and grabbed the candle and the matches.

"I'll tell you the spell; it's really easy. We need to repeat it seven times, and then blow out the candle." Kat looked at me with a big grin on her face. "You know what to do when the flame goes out, right?"

"Imagine our spell becoming one with reality as the smoke mingles with the air," I recited.

"Right. Here's the spell: Grow strong, live long, stand tall, hear the Lady's call."

"That's it?"

"Most spells are simple. Probably so the coven doesn't flub up when they all have to say them at the same time," Kat scoffed. A brisk wind blew through the garden. My hair flew into my face and the pond water rippled. "Hand me the matches. Hurry," she said, "or it's going to be impossible to light the candle. The winds are supposed to be fierce tonight." While Kat lit the wick, I sprinkled sage and jasmine around the tiny seedlings. She cupped her hand around the flame as the warm wind continued to blow.

We repeated the spell seven times, and blew the candle out together. I concentrated on the seeds growing into brilliant flowers as the smoke vanished. Kat's eyes flashed in my direction. "Did you remember?"

"Of course. I pictured nice strong plants with lots of flowers."

"No, DUMMY!" she shouted. I stared at my friend with my mouth open. "You were supposed to imagine *gems*, DUH." She stood up. "Now you've ruined it," she said, glaring at me.

"Maybe you should go." I was completely sick of my rude friend, who was always getting mad and criticizing me.

"Fine." Kat stalked through the gate, looking toward the stables as she walked through the yard. I hoped if Carlos were out there he would ignore her.

I sat down by the pond and stared into the water. *Kat's just another kind of bully*, I realized. *She turns mean and insulting when she doesn't get her way.* As I started to wonder whether or not I wanted to stay friends with her, I noticed a new vine with pinkish-orange blossoms had circled the pond. The male duck with the blue-green head glided over to the edge and nibbled on them. "They may not have gems inside, but at least they're good for something," I muttered, standing up to go back inside the house.

As I walked through the rusty gate, I heard a piercing scream.

36
Real Friends

I ran across the stones and slipped between the pines. On the far side of the yard, Kat sat on the ground holding her ankle. Carlos got there ahead of me and helped her to her feet. He seemed concerned, and I couldn't help thinking that Kat looked triumphant. They hobbled together toward the house, and she looked playfully up at him through her eyelashes as she tried to thank him in Spanish. Kat held onto his hand and giggled as she mispronounced *gracias*. He pulled politely away, heading for the stable. I thought that it served her right that her love potion wasn't working after all.

As soon as Carlos turned his back, Kat stopped limping completely. She hopped on her bike, and then turned around to see if Carlos was watching. After he disappeared inside the stable, she peddled furiously down the street. "What a phony," I said out loud. *Alexa would never do anything like that.* Weighing Kat's good points against her bad ones, I decided that no matter how many cool things she had shown me, they didn't make up for her bossing me around and insulting me.

Suddenly I realized that I couldn't wait another second to talk to my real BFF, and ran across the lawn and into the house. Alexa had texted the night before last that she was home from camp, but we hadn't talked yet. Locking my door as I picked up my phone to call her, I curled up on the alcove seat with a big smile on my face.

"Hello?" Alexa answered.

The second I heard her voice my heart flooded with happiness. "It's me," I announced.

"Me who?" I could tell she was smiling.

"Skylar!"

"Well it's about time," Alexa scolded. "What took you so long to call?"

"Well you couldn't text or talk from camp, and then the last couple days I was busy with summer school and stuff." I knew I was making a lame excuse.

"And all your new friends in Malibu?" I heard the hurt in her voice.

"Ugh," I said, surprising myself with my reaction. "Not even." Tucking my feet underneath me, I launched into the story of Kat and the forgotten garden. I described the buried box with the rusted key, the Ouija board, and the rescued bird.

"Wow," Alexa breathed. "That sounds amazing. No wonder you haven't called me."

"Well you haven't called me either," I reminded her. "How was camp?"

"Fun at first. Then it got boring. How's *Gwendolyn*?"

"We put a hex on her last month and she caught mono. It was going around, but she's stayed away from us ever since. I think she's afraid of Kat."

Alexa giggled. "Typical bully," she said. "Scaredy-cat."

"Exactly. My friend Rudy got in her face when she was rude on the bus and she looked like she was ready to pee her pants."

Alexa laughed out loud. "She's just a chicken in disguise. So what else happened since you've been away?"

"One really bizarre thing." I guess my voice sounded

195

weird, because Alexa whispered when she asked me what happened. "OK. One day Kat and I were about to cast a spell under a weeping willow tree. And then she proved to me how she could control my body by using her energy."

"No way."

"Yes. First she told me to start rotating my foot clockwise."

"Right," Alexa said. I heard a little smile in her voice.

"And then she made my foot change direction, just by concentrating her energy and pointing her finger." I remember the out-of-control feeling I got under the weeping willow when I couldn't stop my foot from turning the other way.

"Let me guess: she told you to make a 6 in the air with your right hand?"

"Wait." I got that creepy feeling again. Like something big was going on behind my back. "How did you know?"

"You fell for that?" Alexa shouted, laughing into the phone. "We did that in Science in third grade! It has something to do with the halves of your brain. You can't help but move your foot to go with your hand."

"What? But no, she…." I shut my mouth. It seemed much more logical to pay attention to Alexa.

"Google, 'circle your foot and make a *six* with your hand.' Oh my God, she really has you fooled!" She giggled some more.

Had Kat deceived me with a simple trick? I couldn't wait to go online and find out exactly how she did it.

"Well, even if that was a trick, a whole bunch of other really weird stuff happened." I told her about the meeting of the coven and sneaking down to the caves at midnight. Demonia drumming in Shadow Hills. I described the seaweed pods, the gem seed spell, the evil in the garden, and the maggot plant we grew.

"Ugh, gross! There were really worms coming out of it?" Alexa shrieked.

"Yes. It was disgusting." I wished Alexa were sleeping over so bad I could have cried. "I miss you so much."

"I miss you too. Shame on both of us for not calling right away," she said, and then got right back to catching up.

"So what's new at home?" I asked, longing to be back on my own street in my own neighborhood, hanging out with my real friends and my family.

"I saw Dustin Coles at the mall." Alexa sounded like she was ready to spill a delicious secret. "He asked where you were."

"He *did*? No way." I snuggled into the cushion, eager to hear more. I'd been crushing on Dustin for two years straight. His sun-streaked hair just touched his collar, and his hazel eyes were so big I melted whenever I looked into them. He was the fastest boy in track and the president of Student Council. *Total* hottie.

"Swear. I told him you went to summer school in Malibu and he thought that was really cool."

"He really said that? Did he say, 'that's cool,' or, 'that's really cool'?"

Alexa laughed. "I'm pretty sure he said, 'Malibu? Wow. That's cool.'"

"Awesome," I said, hugging my pillow and smiling. "And guess what? I'm learning sign language. And I can't wait to teach it to you. Because I read online that signing actually helps people with dyslexia."

"Really?" Alexa's voice got a little higher. "How?"

"The dyslexics that blogged about it said it makes it easier for them to express themselves. And to understand things. Anyway it will be so fun for us to talk in sign language in middle school." I got excited, thinking about starting seventh grade. "No one will know what we're talking about."

"That sounds awesome. I can't wait to learn it."

"There's a hearing-impaired boy in my class," I said, picturing Andy.

"Really? Is he cute?"

"Not so much, but Andy's cool and funny. He has red hair and freckles. Kat calls him a *ginger*."

"She would." Alexa sounded disgusted. "I hate it when people call me that. Your new friend sounds—not very nice."

"You're right," I agreed. "She isn't. But Andy is. I taught myself how to fingerspell and he showed me a few other signs." I thought about my classmates for a minute. "The only other person who really talks to him is a cool guy named Rudy."

"That's sad." Alexa could relate to anybody who had a disability. She hated getting laughed at and knew exactly how bad it felt.

"It is. But Andy's teaching Rudy how to sign too, and he's already way better at it than me. Rudy's the best artist in the whole class. He's really funny, too," I said. *And he's not a dork, no matter what Kat thinks.*

"So, when are you coming home?" Alexa asked.

"Next week's the final and then summer school's over. My parents are coming back on the seventeenth."

"Eleven more days."

It sounded like forever. I looked around my tiny room at the slanted ceiling, the new lock on my door, and the closet where I used to hide my belongings to keep them safe, and I absolutely could not wait to go home.

37
So Much Magic

The next day in art class Kat acted like nothing had happened and she was my best friend again. She dashed off a backward note and tossed it across our desk. I hoped she had thought about how she'd treated me and that the note was an apology.

Wrong.

Did you talk to Carlos?

I didn't bother writing my response backward.

No.

I tossed the piece of paper back at Kat.

Across the room, Rudy Dean was laughing with the other guys at his table. Sue translated for Andy with quick hands and a smile. The cute surfer was texting someone with his cell hidden beneath his desk. One of the popular girls was pointing at him and cracking up. Everybody seemed to be having fun except me. I was starting to wish I had sat at one of their tables on the first day of class instead of choosing to sit by myself, leaving the desk open for Kat. I looked up at Miss Yamato. She was explaining our final exam project.

Kat ignored the instructions and feverishly wrote a backward note, which I read quickly: **I forgive you for messing up the gem spell. We'll try it again later.**

I scribbled a reply, forward.

Whatever.

"For your final project, you can choose a partner or work on your own. The project is up to you. But you must incorporate something you learned in class." I had already decided to ask Rudy to do the final with me when Kat passed me a note.

We'll work together of course.

I answered her right away.

I think I'm going to ask Rudy to work with me this time. No offense.

She didn't look at me for the rest of the period. I was surprised to realize that I really didn't care.

After school I stashed my bike in the garage and headed for the garden. This time Gwendolyn shocked me by standing at the edge of the steppingstone walkway. "Where are you going?" she demanded, blocking my path with her arms folded across her chest.

All of a sudden it didn't seem like such a big deal to keep the forgotten garden a secret. "I'm going to do a little weeding," I admitted. "Want to help?" I opened the gate and stood bravely aside, inviting my cousin to come into my private place.

"Yeah, *right.*" Gwendolyn looked toward her house, laughing loudly, like I was a fool to think she'd ever help me weed the garden.

I finally got my guts up and asked what I'd always wanted to ask. "So Gwendolyn, why do you like picking on me so much?"

Gwendolyn looked around her yard, then over to the goat pen and the stable like she needed help. "I'm not picking on you." Then she took a step toward me and put her hands on her hips. "Why? You scared?"

"Not at all," I said. "I just feel bad for you if the most

fun you have is bugging me. You must be completely bored." I shook my head like my cousin's life was pretty pathetic.

"Not even." Gwendolyn's face turned pink. "I am so not bored," she scoffed, hurrying toward her house like she had a ton of projects to finish. Or like she couldn't get away from me fast enough. She turned to look at me, but this time she wasn't laughing.

I really wished I'd stood up to her sooner. *Years* sooner.

Passing through the gate, I knelt down in front of my new seedlings. I couldn't believe my eyes. The ingredients from the witch's starter kit must have been the strongest fertilizer ever. Most of the seeds had already sprouted. One of the baby stems was almost an inch tall and its first set of leaves had started to form. I wondered how long it would take the flowers to bud, and if there were any chance that something valuable might be inside.

Sitting on the moldy cushion in front of the fountain, I dropped a few sage leaves into what was left of the water. I swirled it clockwise to see if the herbs would offer a clue, but they just drifted aimlessly in the cloudy puddle. Looking around the garden, I realized that nothing I had learned in art class could match the beauty that nature created in the colorful blossoms. All of a sudden my final project became crystal clear. Rudy had partnered with Andy again so I'd decided to work by myself.

I ran inside the house and got a pair of sharp scissors and a basket. Then I headed back to the far corner of the garden. Parting the wide green nasturtium leaves, I cut tangerine-colored blossoms with red-orange streaks, brilliant yellow blooms striped in red, and maroon flowers with magenta splotches. Next I cut a section of the vine that circled the pond. Pretty pink-orange petals bloomed all along its stem. I put it into the basket with the nasturtiums. Continuing through the garden, I snipped lengths of herbs, pink roses, and bright purple flowers from the twiggy plant in the corner.

Back inside the house I opened up my art supplies drawer, pulling out watercolor paints and a pad of good paper. I set up at the kitchen table with a bowl of water to rinse my brush and a roll of paper towels. After arranging the flowers in their basket, I penciled in the negative space I saw between the blossoms. Then I started to paint. I couldn't wait to tell my mom and dad about my summer and show them my artwork.

Aunt Caroline walked into the kitchen a little while later. She admired my painting over my shoulder. "You're really good," she said, impressed. "Where did all those beautiful flowers come from?"

I decided since I was going home soon there really wasn't a reason to keep it secret anymore. "I planted the herbs in this little garden I found behind the pine trees. The nasturtiums, roses, and that skinny plant with the purple flowers were already there."

"You brought Aunt Evelyn's garden back to life. That's wonderful." Aunt Caroline placed a warm hand on my shoulder. I blinked in surprise, remembering Kat's words.

"Whoever planned this garden really knew what she was doing. There's so much magic here!"

Suddenly my heartbeat quickened and there was something I had to ask. "Was Great-Aunt Evelyn into

203

witchcraft?"

Aunt Caroline stared into the hills for a minute before she turned toward me. "Yes. Evvy was very interested in it."

Kat was right.

"She liked anything that had to do with the occult. She used to have this Ouija board. I wonder what ever happened to it?" My aunt tapped her jaw as she thought. "Anyway, she liked to do spells and she was interested in astrology. Are you interested in those things too?"

"A little," I admitted. After swirling my brush in white and then dipping it into orange, I decorated the centers of the burnt orange petals I had just painted.

"Before you go home," Aunt Caroline said, "I'll take you into the attic. I'm sure Evelyn would be delighted that you revived her garden. There are some things of hers up there that I bet she'd want you to have."

"Thanks, Aunt Caroline, that sounds great."

38
Tiny Sparkling Gems

On the last day of school, I walked into art class holding my painting and a photo that Uncle Jim had taken of the basket of flowers. My aunt and uncle couldn't stop telling me how lifelike my watercolor was. Gwendolyn even admitted that it was good.

"Everyone, please set your final projects up on your desks, and I will pass through the room and grade them," Miss Yamato said. "You may walk around and appreciate one another's work as well."

Walking over to Andy and Rudy's table, my mouth fell open. They had made a huge structure using copper wire, scrap metal, and twisted pipe cleaners. Their project showed an angel perching on a mountaintop, aiming a bow and arrow at a demon crouching below.

Andy asked me what I thought of their project, signing as he mouthed the words. "Wha you thih?"

As I was about to answer, Sue stepped up beside him and translated in a clear voice: "What do you think?"

I'd practiced the signs I'd learned online. I signed *wonderful* by showing Andy my palms facing him: low by my waist, then higher up in the air. "Your project is great," I told Rudy Dean, who gave me a bashful smile. Andy read my lips and Sue translated what I said.

Andy touched his fingers to his chin and then lowered his palm. *Thank you.*

"Thank you," Sue interpreted.

"It's OK," I told her, "I can understand him." I pointed

at myself, then flicked my index finger up by my temple.

Andy waved Sue away. "Sylah unnahstan me," Andy said proudly. I bounced my fist for *yes*. His expression told me I was one of the few hearing kids besides Rudy who had actually tried.

When I walked back to my desk I looked at Kat's project. "Yours is really good," I told her. She had decorated several glass candleholders with Wiccan symbols using liquid lead and glass stain.

Kat was really mad when Miss Yamato wouldn't let her light the candles. "But the flames inside make the colors glow," she complained.

"I'm sorry, but I can't allow students to use matches," Miss Yamato said. "Good job. B plus." She noted the grade on her clipboard. Kat glared at her back as the teacher moved over to study my painting.

Kat tapped her foot while she waited for Miss Yamato to grade my project. She was mad that she didn't get an *A* and took it out on me. "I can't believe you're friends with Rudy Beanpole and that deaf *ginger*."

I took a deep breath and decided to stick up for myself again. "I don't really care *what* you think of my friends, Kat," I said. And I meant it. I turned my back before she had a chance to reply. I knew she was giving me a dirty look. Whatever.

"That's a beautiful watercolor, Skylar," Ms. Yamato said. "But what did you incorporate that you learned in this class?"

"The use of negative space." I pointed out the areas between the flowers. "I drew them first, with pencil, before I started to paint. That's why some of the flowers look a little abstract."

"Very good, Skylar. A."

Kat looked back and forth between my painting and me like she was trying to figure out what to say. I could tell by the look in her eyes she was weighing which battle was more important: the other people I'd chosen to be my friends, or if I'd still be one of hers?

I was totally sure that I no longer cared what she thought. I knew who my real friends were and it didn't matter what they looked like. They proved their friendship was real by how they treated me. And about how Kat treated me? I didn't even want to go there.

After Miss Yamato walked away I passed my painting to Kat. I was excited to show her before. Now I was just being polite. "Notice anything?"

She leaned over the paper, studying my final project. Then her eyes widened and she gave me half a smile. In the center of several of the flowers I had painted tiny sparkling gems.

"Can I have that?" Kat asked. "It would go perfect in my earth quadrant."

I looked at my final project. I'd spent hours on it. It was the best thing I'd made all year, and I was really proud of it. I was looking forward to hanging it up in my bedroom, once I was finally home.

"I'll trade you," Kat said. She pointed at the candle-holders she'd decorated with symbols of the four elements, pentagrams, and zodiac signs.

"Um," I said, stalling. I didn't want to give away my painting. Then I remembered how Kat had rescued me from a summer of loneliness. Taught me tons of cool things about witchcraft. Showed me how to stand up for myself against bullies like Gwendolyn. And pushed me to conquer my biggest fear. I loved horseback riding now, thanks to her.

"Can't you see it? Hanging above my plants and candles?" Kat looked at me expectantly.

"Yeah I can." I lowered the arm holding my picture down by my side. I still didn't want to let it go. "Thank you for teaching me everything you did. The flowers we grew—at the end—were really beautiful."

Kat's whole face scrunched. "You're thanking me for gardening tips? Those lousy flowers were worthless. Are you kidding me?" She shook her head and gave me *the look*. "What about introducing you to everything Wiccan?" Kat put her hands on her hips and stared at me like I really had something big to thank her for.

"About everything Wiccan?" I thought about it for a minute. "I'm really not sure."

My painting symbolized everything that had happened in the forgotten garden. The gem seed spell, the magic. The trust and mistrust. The maggots and the smell of rot. Suddenly I really didn't even want to touch it anymore. I handed her my painting.

It felt good to let it go.

39
Rescue

After dinner I started to pack. Pulling my detective kit from under the bed, I popped the dusty Nanta bag into it. I was looking forward to showing it to Alexa, and hearing her laugh at witchcraft and tease me about the things I'd been afraid of. When I sent her the picture Carlos had taken of me on Brownie's back, I got an excited text back from my BFF:

Congrdualtons on facing ur fers!

Alexa always knew what I was feeling no matter how far apart we were. I decided that worrying about Demonia was a waste of time, and the people who did needed to get a clue.

That night I found out just how wrong I was.

Outside the alcove window, a full moon blazed bright, lighting up the backyard in a milky glow. The wind howled fiercely, slamming the oak tree branches against my window, making it rattle and moan. My skin felt itchy and my hair was full of static, floating out around my head like it couldn't lie still. I crammed my art supplies into my suitcase quickly, feeling like I needed to hurry.

My aunt and uncle went out to see a movie. Before they left they cautioned Gwendolyn and me to be careful like they always did, but this time they seemed just a little bit frantic. My uncle checked and rechecked the alarm system, twisting the back door handle more than once to make sure it was locked. I caught Caroline staring out the kitchen window into Shadow Hills, fretting her fingers. When she noticed me watching her she smiled like nothing was wrong.

But something was wrong.

The wind ripped through the mountains, drying out Malibu with brittle, dusty gusts. I looked up into the mountainside as I packed my clothes. The bright moonlight made the shadows seem deeper, darker than the rest of the hillside. Twisted oak branches creaked and popped like arms that were about to break off. Turning away from the window and heading for my slanted closet, I wished I had blinds I could close. Something that would block out the fierce night.

Down in Gwendolyn's goat pen the animals were restless, bleating loudly. I shoved clothes I knew I wouldn't wear again into my suitcase, searching the closet floor in case anything had fallen off a hanger. Lifting the lid off the third hatbox from which Gwendolyn had stolen my diary, I made sure it was empty. Then I heard a noise that made my blood curdle: an inhuman scream, high and shrieking.

Grabbing my binoculars, I kneeled on the alcove seat and stared out the window. The yard was dark and silent. Pulling out my cell, I texted Alexa.

R U there? I'd call but don't want any1 2 hear. Something really bad happens in the hills at night. Just hrd animals screaming. Or maybe ppl. R U home?

No reply. My knees ground into the window seat's cushion as I got closer to the glass and focused my binoculars. And then I leaned even closer. Up in the hills, a ring of fire burned close to the ground. Shadowy shapes hunched around the flames, darker than the moonlit hill behind them. They moved quickly around the fire as if they were dancing. Celebrating after someone had screamed. Something evil was definitely happening in Shadow Hills. Now I'd seen it with my own eyes. *But what was it?*

Then I heard that horrible noise again. A throaty howl, like an animal in terror. Moments later feet pounded down the hall to my room. Gwendolyn burst through my door without knocking. "Skylaryouhavetodosomething!" she shouted. My cousin's face was red and blotchy. She clenched and unclenched her hands in panic. "Someone's stealing Shena!"

Jumping up onto the window seat and aiming my binoculars toward the right side of the yard, I saw a figure in a black robe bending over the fenced-in goat pen. Shena screamed again as the robed figure snatched her up, dumping her into a wheelbarrow. Then a needle glinted in the moonlight and Shena collapsed like she'd gone to sleep. For once my cousin was right. A thief had just drugged a goat and was stealing her right out of our backyard.

"Call 9-1-1," I shouted. "Hurry!"

"Don't let them get away!" Gwendolyn screamed, bursting into tears. "That's my goat," she sobbed, as I scrambled into my jacket. "You have to rescue her! *Please* Skylar!" Opening my Porta-detective kit, I dumped the contents into my backpack and put it on.

Cramming my cell into my pocket, I stared into Gwendolyn's panicked face and grabbed her by the shoulders. "Call 9-1-1," I repeated. Then I ran down the stairs, through the kitchen, and into the dark backyard.

The robed figure wheeled Shena through the pines and disappeared. There was something funny about his walk. Maybe he was hobbling because of the wheelbarrow. No time to figure it out now. I knew he was heading for Shadow Hills. And I thought I knew what he planned to do with Shena.

Witches. Bruja. Goats. Sacrifice.

I had to find a way to save her.

The other goats bleated loudly. Wind screamed through the backyard, making it hard to walk. Grabbing my hair to keep it out of my eyes, I pitched across the grounds toward the stable, praying that Carlos was home. When I finally reached the guesthouse I pounded on the door. I strained to hear if someone was coming but the howling wind drowned out anything I could have heard.

Finally, Rosa opened the door, but just a few inches. *"¿Qué pasó?"* What is it?

"Carlos *por favor!*" She turned and called his name. He peeked out of his bedroom, then hurried up to me like he had been waiting. "Someone just stole Shena. Thief!" I cried, pointing toward the pen, hoping he understood.

"*¿Bruja?*" he asked, and I shook my head. Not a witch.

"A man. *Hombre,*" I said, remembering what Kat said about covens usually having twelve women and one man.

"*Brujo,*" Carlos said. *Warlock.*

"Hurry," I urged, but he was already rushing past me, heading for the stables. I followed him into the gusty backyard. The wind tore at my hair and made my eyes water. I plowed forward, following Carlos. Stealing a glance up into Shadow Hills, I saw a dark, hulking figure lurching up the path. Next to us, the older goats screamed for their missing kid. The air was filled with panic.

Waiting for Carlos to saddle Brownie, the wind made my nose sting and run so badly I could hardly breathe. Carlos finally came out of the stable on Lightning's bare back, leading Brownie by her bridle. He had some thick rope coiled around his shoulder. "*¡Rapido!*" he shouted, tossing the reins down to me. *Hurry!*

It didn't matter that it was pitch dark, and a coven was plotting to use black magic against us. There was a helpless animal's life at stake. I didn't care that it was Gwendolyn's. I just needed to rescue it from Demonia and its fate up in Shadow Hills. I stuck my foot in the stirrup and swung my other leg up and over Brownie's back without even thinking.

Carlos kicked Lightning's sides and she took off running. Brownie trotted after her, then accelerated into a canter. I could barely make out the robed figure, leaning into the wind and pushing something heavy up the path into the mountains: a wheelbarrow, holding Shena.

The night was so dark I could hardly see the ground, but a dull red glow lit up the pockets of the hillside. As the shadows danced, a big bird screeched by my head, startling me and spooking the horses. A crow. Beyond the shrieking wind and the cawing bird I heard voices chanting.

Carlos whistled and Brownie surged forward. Wrapping my hands around the reins, I squeezed her sides with my legs like my life depended on it. It probably did. Air gusted past my ears, making a shuddering noise as it flapped the leaves on the trees. We started up the path. Brownie's mane whipped in front of my face and I struggled to see past it into the dark hillside.

We climbed higher up the mountain and the breeze whistled and moaned. I coughed as dust blew into my mouth and up my nose. We rounded a bend and I spotted the man in the shadows ahead of us. Carlos reined Lightning as we neared the shadowed figure, and Brownie's trot slowed to a walk.

The warlock turned right, hobbling into a cave, pushing the heavy wheelbarrow. *Shena*, I though desperately. *What is he about to do to her?*

Carlos steered Lightning to the left, heading higher up the hill. He looked over his shoulder, putting a finger to his lips. As if the coven could hear us over the wind. Like I could even speak if I wanted to. Breathing and not panicking was taking up all the room in my brain.

Brownie huffed, jerking her head side to side, making it hard for me to hang onto the reins. But we had to climb further. *Then we can look down and see what they're doing.* The hillside got steeper. The horses panted like they were thirsty. Dirt blew around us, making it even harder to breathe. At the bottom of the hill, lights glowed behind a window in Gwendolyn's house. How I wished I were safely tucked inside the rose room, curled up with my diary in the alcove seat, out of the wind and danger. Where the only shadows were real ones, made by light bulbs. My aunt's house seemed far away, like a distant dream.

All of a sudden I realized couldn't see or hear Lightning any longer. Kicking my heels into Brownie's sides, I pushed her to go faster. I'd lost sight of Carlos. If I got stranded in the mountains with Demonia and a horse that badly needed a drink—I didn't want to think about it. Straining to hear Lightning over the roaring wind, I urged Brownie farther up the mountain.

40
Demonia

Around the next bend there was a pocket of shadow and a white horse, hiding. "*Aqui*," Carlos whispered. *Here.* Steering Brownie by her reins, we shuffled up next to Lightning. The horses snorted and stomped their feet, trying to get comfortable on the unstable hillside in the crackling air. Carlos leaned toward me, pointing down into Shadow Hills.

One level down, dark-cloaked figures surrounded a squirming bundle. Whatever the warlock had shot into Shena was wearing off. The little goat was starting to wake up. A skinny witch grabbed Shena by the scruff of her neck and dragged her toward their flickering fire.

Around the flaming circle, the witches danced sideways with their arms linked together. One of them would shriek, and the others would belt back an answer, chanting in a language I couldn't understand. The warlock tipped his head up to the sky and shouted a command. The witches danced faster. They chanted louder. Something was about to happen.

What are they going to do to Shena? I thought desperately, remembering the burnt bones I'd seen last time, and her liquid brown eyes looking up at me. *We have to save her!*

Carlos tied a slipknot in one end of the rope, making a lasso. Pointing at the members of the coven, he said something to me in Spanish that I didn't get. I shrugged, so he made waving motions with his hands, like he wanted me to distract them. Looking down at Demonia, I knew what I had to do. Reaching into my backpack, I pulled out my penlight and turned it on.

Aiming it down the hillside onto the clearing, I jiggled the light around the witches' feet. They had thought they were alone and it freaked them out. One jumped back and another one screeched. "Now!" I shouted at Carlos, hoping he would understand.

He did, and raised the lasso high over his head, twirling it around and around, focusing on Shena's little body while I aimed my penlight down at her. The witches all looked up the hillside to see where the light was coming from.

Then the shadows shifted. The group bent their heads together like they were conferring about something. Or praying. Or planning an attack. They danced around the fire again, bellowing in unison. It wasn't English or Spanish. It sounded like they were talking backward. The eerie words sounded ghoulish and evil. Flames from the fire lit up their faces. The women were skinny with dark, ragged clothing and messy hair. They didn't look neat or professional, like my mom or my aunt. They didn't look like any type of moms at all.

The warlock darted into a cave and came out holding a metal tool. It looked like a little shovel with a long handle. Scooping it into the fire, he pulled out a red-hot coal. He lobbed it up at us as the witches cackled and screamed. They picked up stones and threw them up at us. The wind gusted and the weeds around the horses' feet burst into flames. Lightning pawed the ground, snorting, and Carlos swore in Spanish, grabbing his ankle.

"Are you OK?" I shrieked.

Carlos slapped at the bottom of his pant leg. His jeans were on fire. He spit out a rapid stream of loud Spanish that I didn't understand.

Another burning coal landed near us and Brownie reared up on her hind legs. I hung onto the reins and the saddle's horn, trying desperately not to slide off her back. She pawed the hot air with her front hooves and I tried not to scream.

Carlos was hurt. He reached for his leg and winced. His dark eyes flashed at me, angry and scared. The warlock had burned my friend.

I was furious. Shaking the hair out of my face, I glared at Carlos, pointing down at the coven and then making a fist. We needed stronger weapons. Time to fight fire with fire.

I took out my laser light and turned it on. *My mom always worried that I would blind myself or someone else with it, but I kept it in case I was ever chased by robbers or someone I needed to blind to save my life.*

If there was ever a time to use it, it was now.

As the warlock took aim at us again I shined my laser light down at his face, pointing it into his eyes. He let out a high-pitched shriek and staggered forward, favoring his left leg. *Something familiar about him,* I thought, glancing into my backpack and wishing I had a better weapon. The warlock looked up at us, reaching into the fire for another red-hot coal. I aimed my laser at his face again.

He screamed and bent over, grabbing his eyes as my laser light bobbed and danced around him. *Was I really trying to blind another human being?* I thought desperately. *No. I'm protecting myself,* my conscience answered as another dry bush exploded into flames near Brownie's feet. *And if he's throwing fireballs at us on a windy night and they catch the hillside on fire and burn the horses or us, he deserves what he gets.* Just then the breeze blew the hood off the warlock's head, revealing pale, stringy hair.

I recognized him.

It was Dilbert, the clerk from Malibu Curios & Souvenirs. While his screams were swallowed up by the wind, Carlos lassoed Shena.

Brownie reared back on her hind legs braying loudly and my stomach rose up into my throat. I felt like I was on an elevator that went into free fall, and I hung on for my life. The wind howled and the fire spread, igniting the bushes around us. Brownie and Lightning whinnied and stomped, desperate to escape the heat and flames.

The coven was relentless, heaving fireballs and rocks up at us one after the other. My laser light hadn't done any damage. Over the whistling of the wind I heard fierce voices chanting. Demonia was trying to hex Carlos and me. Brownie. Shena. My family.

Carlos tugged on the rope and made a clicking sound with his tongue, coaxing Shena toward us. The little goat scrambled up the hillside while I aimed my laser light into anyone's eyes who tried to snatch her up. Witches grabbed at their faces and turned away. Some of them screamed and ran into a cave. "I know who you are, Dilbert!" I shouted. "You work at Malibu Curios!" Then I aimed my penlight at him and flicked it on and off as if I had taken his picture. "And now I can prove it!" Dilbert ducked his head and limped into the cave.

Carlos motioned at me. Time to go. Trees ignited above us and the blaze surged through the dry branches over our heads. Flames danced as more of the hillside caught fire. The wind gusted and hot sparks ignited Shadow Hills. Burning brush crackled and popped. Tumbleweeds and dead bushes blazed all around the horses' feet. Witches pitched rocks at me as the fire spread around us. The wind moaned. And then it changed direction.

When the wind shifted, the fire ripped down the hillside toward the coven. I heard shrieks as the bushes outside of their circle caught fire. The flames roared as they raced up the dry trees, jumping from limb to limb until there was a burning forest raging around us. Demonia was forced to retreat into the shadows.

The blaze spread. The heat was extreme. It was so hot I thought I would melt into Brownie's saddle. Bending forward into the wind, I rode down the steep path behind Carlos, watching Shena as she trotted next to Lightning. When I looked at the scorched ring where the coven had been standing, it was empty. Demonia was gone.

Then I heard another noise: *Wup, wup, wup,* sounded from way above us. The ground lit up around Brownie's feet. A strong light shined down at us. A fire department helicopter circled overhead.

Someone important knew Malibu was on fire.

41
Escape

I looked over my shoulder. The flames were chasing us down the hillside. Carlos urged the horses forward and Shena ran as fast as she could by his side. When we got to the bottom of the mountain I turned around and looked up. Shadow Hills were blazing. Thick black smoke rose into the air and disappeared against the night sky. A second 'copter circled. *Wump, wump, wump.*

Carlos held Lightning to a trot so Shena could keep up. When we finally rode back into Gwendolyn's yard she was standing by the stream waiting for us. "Shena!" she screamed when she saw Carlos and his rope leash. Tears ran down her cheeks as we led Shena and the horses over to her. While they gulped water from the stream, I swung my leg over Brownie's back, anxious to stand on solid ground again. Then Gwendolyn shocked me. She grabbed me in a sweaty hug for the first time ever. "Thank you so much," she sobbed, reaching down to hug her pet. She smothered the goat's face with kisses as a dry tree exploded on the hillside.

"*¡Vamos!* We go!" Carlos said, motioning for me to get back on the horse's back. "No safe. Fire coming," he said, pointing to the back of the yard.

Gwendolyn looked at the guesthouse. "Carlos's parents were screaming for him. I kept pointing at the stable and into Shadow Hills. Rosa was crying but they finally got in their car and left."

"*¿Mi madre?*" Carlos asked, panic in his eyes.

Gwendolyn made steering motions with her hands and pointed down the hill. "Your parents left," she said.

Bright orange flames leaped up from the hillside behind the pines. If the fire wasn't put out soon, Gwendolyn's house could burn down. "Did you call 9-1-1?" I shouted over the roar of the helicopter.

Gwendolyn bobbed her head. "I told the police someone stole Shena and then I called 9-1-1 again when I smelled smoke."

"Good job," I said as the wind blew my hair into my eyes. "We have to get out of here. The fire could spread before they get it under control."

Someone echoed my idea. A man's voice boomed through a megaphone and a flashing red beacon lit up Gwendolyn's street. "Attention residents: This is a *mandatory* evacuation. Take your pets and leave the area immediately. If you are on foot, cross Pacific Coast Highway and wait on the sand until the fire is out. Repeat: This is a *mandatory* evacuation."

"I'm not leaving my goats!" Gwendolyn screamed. The wind howled. Smoke poured into her backyard, choking the animals and making it impossible to breathe.

"Then leash them up," I said, coughing. "Hurry!"

"*¡Rapido!*" Carlos shouted as Lightning pawed the ground, shaking her head from side to side.

The smoke was getting thicker. The fire was getting closer.

Gwendolyn rushed into the goat pen and pulled the lasso off Shena's neck. "Help me!" she yelled, and Carlos jumped off of Lightning's back. *Wup, wup, wup,* sounded from above us. The helicopter's floodlight illuminated the

222

yard, the stable, and the goat pen. Moments later Carlos had all four goats tethered together.

"I take goats, you take her," Carlos told me, pointing at Gwendolyn. "We go to beach. *¡Ahora!" Now!* He looked at me and pointed at Brownie.

"Can you get on behind me?" I asked my cousin, putting my foot into the stirrup and hoisting myself up into the saddle.

"I don't have a choice," Gwendolyn grumbled as an ear-splitting siren screamed past her house. "I have to call my mom," she said, looking at the horse, then at her phone, and back at me, her cheeks wet with tears.

"Get on. We need to get out of here. You can call her later." I reached my hand down to my cousin. She waited one second before grabbing it. Gwendolyn stepped into the stirrup and I pulled her up onto Brownie's back behind me. "Hang on to me so you don't slide off," I said, but Gwendolyn hesitated. "It's OK," I urged her, "it's an emergency." My cousin finally wrapped her arms around me.

Carlos clicked his tongue, and Lightning trotted through the yard with four goats running by her side and Brownie and two riders following.

42
Malibu on Fire

The wind shrieked and whistled and the air was thick with smoke. Gwendolyn let go of me with one hand and I heard tiny beeps. "Mom!" she cried. "The hills are on fire right behind our house. I called 9-1-1." She was quiet for a minute. Then, "Carlos has the goats and we're riding the horses to the beach. You better come home!" I heard Gwendolyn sob as she put her arm back around my waist.

Now two helicopters circled over our heads. A cop car passed us, its siren screaming. By the time we reached the sand it seemed like half of Malibu had been evacuated to the beach.

Carlos rode Lightning up to the lifeguard tower and stopped. Jumping down, he wrapped the reins around the tower's leg, tying the rope in a knot. Brownie followed, carrying Gwendolyn and me over to Lightning. Clear air blew across the ocean, and it finally got easier to breathe. I handed Brownie's reins to Carlos and he tied her to the tower too. Then he helped Gwendolyn down and handed her the goats' leashes. Squatting by their sides, my cousin hugged Shena and Sheba, and pet their mom and dad, trying to calm them.

My phone chirped a minute later. It was a text from Kat.

Where r u?

Beach. By 7th lifeguard tower. On a horse. U?

Close. Coming ur way.

More and more people pulled into the beach parking lot or walked up and gathered in groups on the sand. Some held their pets in their arms or had them on leashes or in cages. Other people talked frantically on their cells. A businessman in a suit stood near us, shouting into two different phones, one against each ear. Looking around from up on Brownie's back, I spotted Rudy Dean's head above the rest of the crowd and waved. He smiled and headed over to us. "Some fire, huh?" he said, looking up toward the hills behind Gwen's house.

"Yeah it is. The flames are practically in our backyard. That's why we brought the animals down." I swung my leg over Brownie's back and jumped to the ground like I'd been doing it for years. The first thing I did was walk up to Shena and pet her between the ears. Her big brown eyes looked up at me and she rubbed her head against my hand. Gwendolyn looked at me for a second and I wondered if she was going to remind me that I wasn't allowed to pet her goat, but she just copied me, rubbing Sheba between her ears and then scratching her back.

Kat hurried over to me, followed by Diana and Devon. The wind gusted and they covered their eyes as sand sprayed across the beach. "You actually got back on a horse?" Kat asked with an amused look on her face.

I nodded like it was no big deal. Even though it totally was. "Carlos gave me lessons."

"Hi Carlos," Kat said, smiling at him and ignoring Rudy and me.

"Good thinking, taking the animals," Rudy said, ignoring Kat right back. "My dog's in my dad's car." He looked at the parking lot as another fire engine screamed up into the hills.

My cell chirped with another text. Alexa this time.

R U OK? News shows Malbu on fier!

"Who was that?" Kat asked, like she was annoyed that I got a text from someone besides her.

The wind shifted again and a last gust of smoke clouded the sand. I covered my nose with my sleeve and looked away. Then a wave rolled in, a moist ocean breeze picked up, and the air cleared. "My BFF Alexa," I answered.

Just as I noticed the angry look in Kat's eyes, there was a loud burst up in Shadow Hills. Then another one.

"Oh!" Diana exclaimed, as the fire grew brighter. "Look." She pointed up into hills, muttering a spell under her breath.

"It looks like—the shadows are exploding," Kat said. Rudy and I followed her gaze. Bright pockets of light crackled like fireworks, then burned right out.

"Those aren't real shadows," Diana said. "They never were. They're pockets of Demonia's energy."

Devon looked at me and rolled his eyes. Then he shook his head like he couldn't believe his sister was talking such nonsense.

"I think it's just a bunch of posers who need to get a life," I said.

"What's popping and exploding then?" Diana demanded, glaring at me.

"Dry brush and tumbleweeds."

"Think what you want," Diana snapped. "*I* know the truth."

"So do I," I said, looking her in the eye. "I was just up there." Rudy and Devon nodded. They had my back.

"Kat. You know who the *warlock* is? Demonia's leader? It's that clerk, Dilbert, from the souvenir shop."

"No *way*. You're making that up," Kat snapped.

"I'm not. He had that same high-pitched voice and the bad leg. It was him. I'm positive." Kat shook her head and gave me a disgusted stare, which I ignored. "That explains why he was giving you dirty looks in the store," I continued. "He probably knows you're Diana's sister. Wister's his enemy, remember? It makes perfect sense."

"Why would a warlock need to clerk in a souvenir shop?" Kat demanded. "That doesn't make any sense at all."

"You have the question backward," I said. Devon, Diana, Kat, Carlos, and Rudy were all looking at me, waiting for me to make my point. "It's not, 'why would a warlock need to clerk in a souvenir shop?' It's, 'why would a clerk pretend to be a warlock?'"

"Only a loser who had no life would *pretend* to be a warlock," Kat argued. "You have it all wrong."

"No I don't," I said. "You just explained it perfectly."

Kat looked at me. She thought about it until her lips parted. Then she clenched her teeth and put her hands on her hips. But she couldn't think of anything to say.

Diana dismissed my explanation with a wave of her thin hand, acting like I'd said nothing at all. "Wister is finally winning," she said, gazing up into Shadow Hills.

"You call this winning?" Gwendolyn snapped. "My house could burn down!"

"Moist air's probably helping," Rudy commented, looking at the mountainside. "They should get it put out soon."

The black smoke was turning to gray.

"It's over," Diana said, smiling. "Demonia is gone. I can feel it. I *know* it."

"What are you talking about?" Gwendolyn asked, bending down to calm Shena and Sheba who were still spooked by the noise and the tension in the air.

"You've never heard of Dem—oh, it figures," Kat said, and Gwendolyn glared at her.

But Diana just kept smiling. "Demonia's energy is burning out with the fire. They'll have to leave Shadow Hills now."

Devon shook his head again. "They'll have to leave because they'll get blamed for setting the fire," he said. "Duh."

I remembered Dilbert lobbing fireballs at us and the ring of fire burned into the earth. *Evidence*, I thought. *They* will *have to leave.* I wondered if Dilbert had left his tool behind, and if I could lift his fingerprints off of it.

As I thought this, a wave rolled in and crashed, and the breeze off the dark ocean carried away the last of the smoke. Now all I smelled was the freshness of the sea, like the fire had been nothing but a bad dream. Kat and Diana could believe an evil coven had started the Shadow Hills fire and that Wister had conquered their enemy if they wanted to. It didn't matter to me. Everything and everyone I cared about was safe.

I'm OK now, I texted Alexa. Call u when I get home.

I looked at Diana and remembered when she walked into Kat's room, wearing a cape and clutching her *Book of Shadows*. She needed to get a life as much as Dilbert did.

I was starting to realize what this group of witches and warlocks really were: shallow people who badly needed something to believe in. As if she read my mind, Diana told Devon and Kat to come with her and stalked off across the sand. Devon looked at me over his shoulder and waved. "Bye Devon," I mouthed.

"You coming back to Malibu Middle in fall, new girl?" Rudy Dean asked.

I looked at Kat and Diana's backs and at the smoldering Shadow Hills, and shook my head. "I don't think so."

Rudy's smile faded. He looked at the ocean, then back at me. "You on Facebook?"

"Yeah I am." I tipped my head to one side, smiling like Rudy did on the first day of school. "Skylar Robbins, not New Girl."

Rudy shoved his hands in his pockets, looking serious. Like he was going to miss me. "Friend me?"

"Definitely," I said. "You post pictures of your drawings on FB?" Rudy nodded. "Can't wait to see the next one." I looked way up into his face, and smiled.

"Andy's on Facebook too. Dude has like a thousand friends." He shook his head, looking out across the dark ocean.

"I'll friend him too," I said. "I'll be 1001."

We stood around for another half an hour, waiting for the fire to go completely out. I texted Alexa and chatted with Rudy while Gwendolyn pet the goats and talked to her mom on her cell. Carlos sat on Lightning's back, staring up into Shadow Hills with a worried look on his face, probably wondering where his parents were. Finally a helicopter circled, and I heard another voice boom out of a bullhorn: "The fire is contained. Mandatory evacuation is now lifted. Residents with proof of address can return to their homes. Repeat: evacuation is now lifted."

"Stay real, Skylar," Rudy said, bumping my knuckles before he loped across the sand toward the parking lot.

Gwendolyn's phone rang. She answered, then touched my arm. "My parents are back. They'll meet us at the bottom of the hill with ID so we can prove we live up there." She looked at Carlos. "Your mom and dad are OK." Gwendolyn gave him a thumbs up in case he didn't understand, and Carlos smiled. The relief I felt showed on his face.

"Come on," Gwendolyn said, gathering up the goats' leashes. "We can go home."

43
Whispered Answers

The next morning Aunt Caroline made French toast and bacon for breakfast. She told Gwendolyn and me that we deserved a special treat for practically saving all of Malibu with our quick thinking. I didn't get in trouble for riding up into Shadow Hills like I thought I would. Aunt Caroline said if it hadn't been for me they could have lost their horses and goats, not to mention their house. Gwendolyn nodded all the while, giving me credit I couldn't believe she thought I deserved.

The Malibu blaze was front-page news. Careless campers were suspected of setting the fire. The article didn't say anything about witches, warlocks, or covens. Arson investigators were combing Shadow Hills for clues. The only trace they'd found so far was a black circle burned deep into the scorched earth. The wind continued to blow, covering the char with dead leaves and dust. It wasn't long until it looked like no one had ever been there at all.

The day after the fire I left my bedroom door unlocked, rode my bike down the hill, and found a pay-phone. I placed an anonymous call to the police. I didn't want to get hauled in for questioning, but I needed to tell them what I knew.

"Malibu P.D. Help you?" a bored voice asked.

"Yes, I have information concerning the fire."

"Your name please?"

I ignored the question. "I was horseback riding in the

hills yesterday with a friend. A man named Dilbert who clerks at the souvenir shop near Trancas market scooped burning coals out of a campfire and threw them at us. He started the fire."

"How old are you?" she asked suspiciously.

"Old enough to know that if you find a small shovel and dust it for fingerprints, they will match Dilbert's at Malibu Curios and Souvenirs. That's all I know. I have to go." I started to hang up.

"Wait! What's your name, ma'am? We need any further information you have. There's a reward—"

"Look for a metal shovel and dust it for prints. They'll be Dilbert's," I repeated, and hung up the phone. I didn't want to stay in Malibu a second longer than I had to. Knowing that I had solved the mystery was reward enough.

Two days later I followed Aunt Caroline up the hidden staircase. "Now watch your step," she said. "It's dark and messy up here." I'd sneaked Great-Aunt Evelyn's Ouija board into its hiding spot earlier, putting everything back exactly as I'd found it so my aunt wouldn't figure out I had been inside the attic. She opened the door and we walked into the gloomy room. "Maybe if we open this little window it will be easier to breathe," she said, easing it open. "Now let's see what's in these boxes that you might like to have." Aunt Caroline sliced open the top of the first box of Evelyn's belongings.

The tape split apart invitingly and I looked in at her things. Right on top there was a thick, leather-covered book with a label on the front: *Evelyn's Book of Shadows.*

Kat's voice echoed in my mind: "It's her personal *Book of Shadows*. All witches keep one; it's a record of her journey to the next level."

So Great-Aunt Evelyn was *a witch*. "I'd really like to have that," I said. *I'd really like to analyze that*, I thought. Then I looked around the attic floor and had to ask a question. "What happened to Great-Aunt Evelyn's ashes?"

"What happened to them? Nothing Skylar, they're in their urn on the mantle in my bedroom where they've always been. Why do you ask?"

"Um—Gwendolyn said—never mind."

By the time we were through I had an armload of cool things, including the Ouija board. There was an astrology book, one called *Magic Herb Gardens*, and Evelyn's *Book of Shadows*. My aunt carried a narrow box full of old candles and incense, and a small felt bag of colored crystals with a booklet explaining their powers. Even though I had lost my faith in witchcraft, it would still be fun to teach Alexa how to use the Oujia board and to ask it questions about Dustin Coles. Like how many of my classes would he be in next semester? I couldn't wait to see Dustin again!

"Your parents should be here soon," Aunt Caroline said, leading the way back down the hidden staircase.

"I know. My mom just texted me from the car."

"Are you finished packing?"

"Yes. All my stuff is in the entryway."

I crammed Great-Aunt Evelyn's things into my suitcase. "Hey, what happened to the spiderwebs?" I asked, looking up at the clean skylight.

"Jim finally got on a ladder with a dust mop." Aunt Caroline and I looked at each other and laughed as my parents' car finally pulled into the driveway. I flung open the front door and ran down the driveway to meet them.

My dad swooped me up in a bear hug. "How's my girl?" he asked with a big smile crinkling his eyes.

"Great," I said. Then I hugged my mom—so hard and so long that we both had tears in our eyes when we stepped apart. "So how was Europe?" I asked.

"It was wonderful, Honey, how was your summer?" My mom kept her hand on my shoulder like she didn't want to stop touching me.

"Actually it was really fun, and very—interesting." *You wouldn't believe what I went through in a million years.* "Can I show them the garden before we leave?" I asked my aunt.

"Of course you can. Lead the way."

We walked past the stream, which was gurgling happily. I led them through the pine trees, down the steppingstones, and through the metal gate. Uncle Jim followed us and even Gwendolyn trailed behind.

"Skylar!" Aunt Caroline exclaimed, walking into the garden. "It hasn't looked this beautiful since Evvy was alive."

My mom wandered around the garden. She bent down now and then to take a whiff of a flower or rub a sprig of an herb between her fingers. She sniffed her fingertips. "Mmm—sage. I never knew you were interested in gardening," my mom said, looking at me with a happy smile on her face.

"I never knew I was either," I said, checking on my new

nasturtium shoots. Some of them had brightly colored buds on them, and one deep red bloom had just opened. I didn't think for one second that the flowers would have gems inside, and I found it funny now that I had ever believed they would. I picked the red nasturtium and stuck the spicy blossom behind my ear. "Will someone water the garden after I leave?" I asked, suddenly worried that all of my new flowers would end up dying of thirst.

Then I couldn't believe my ears. "I will," Gwendolyn offered.

"Really?" I looked at her doubtfully.

"This place is really neat," she admitted, looking around. "I'd like to come back here and read. It's nice and private." For once I thought she was telling the truth.

"That would be great," I said, smiling at her for real. As I looked at Gwendolyn, I realized that she had lost a lot of weight while she had been sick with mono. Maybe she was feeling better about herself and would start being nicer to other people now. Plus, surviving the fire and rescuing Shena together had made us closer than we'd ever been.

As we walked across the steppingstones, I took one last look into the forgotten garden. I gazed at the crumbling chalice, the sparkling pond, and that shadowed place where Kat discovered Great-Aunt Evelyn's buried box. I had gone through so much since I first stepped inside those overgrown walls. I'd faced my fears and found courage I never knew I had. Not only had I finally gotten on a horse, I'd ridden one to save another animal's life. And risked mine to take down a coven. Or some lonely people who pretended to be witches and warlocks to make their lives feel more exciting.

Detective Skylar definitely wasn't chicken anymore. I'd stood up to bullies, forgiven my cousin, and realized who my real friends were. I'd grown up a lot. I took a last look inside the beautiful, wild garden, and closed the rusty gate.

44
Treasure in the Vines

I hugged my aunt and uncle as my dad mounted my bike on the back of the car. Gwendolyn and I waved at each other, and then I climbed into the backseat. My detective kit was safe in the trunk with my suitcase and art projects. Great-Aunt Evelyn's box rested on the seat next to me. We all waved goodbye as my dad pulled out of the driveway.

When we finally stopped talking about their trip and my summer, I pulled a note out of my backpack pocket. Kat passed it to me on the last day of school after I gave her my painting. I unfolded it and read the backward writing again.

I hope you come back next summer. Diana's helping me work on a big new spell. We're going to contact Evelyn's spirit and see what else she buried in the garden. Diana says she thinks there is buried treasure back there! And she did a Tarot card reading: There's fortune in the future of a 1—Sky, that's you!

I had stopped believing in the power of witchcraft. The love potion hadn't worked on Carlos. Gwendolyn could have caught mono without our help. The disgusting maggot plant that was supposed to be gems…. I had started to think my dad and Devon were right and that it was mumbo jumbo, mysticism, baloney.

I realized that I'd actually like to try the gem seed spell again—if I could rig a hidden camera to record what happened. Then I could analyze it later, and see what had been going on behind my back. The moans, the rumbling earth, the giggle in the bushes. Was Kat able to throw her voice? Wouldn't surprise me.

I thought about the other friends I'd made this summer. Tall, shy Rudy Dean, the best artist I'd ever met. Hearing-impaired, gentle Andy, who I'd barely gotten to know, partly because of Kat. And my cousin Gwendolyn, who had finally stopped acting like a bully. I wasn't afraid of her anymore. Even if Gwendolyn didn't become my best bud, at least we could be nice to each other like cousins should be. Maybe there was room enough for both of us inside the garden walls.

While I thought about it all, I pulled the baby nasturtium from behind my ear. I ran my fingertips across its velvety softness. Then I bent my head to sniff it and almost jumped off the backseat. Closing my eyes, I shook my head to clear it. Staring at the flower, I snapped my mouth shut. I *had* seen what I thought I'd seen.

In the very center, between the burgundy petals, there was a tiny chip of something bright and red and sparkling. I stared at the baby ruby silently for so long I was sure my mom would turn around and look at me at any second. I tore my eyes off the tiny gem and stashed the blossom inside Great-Aunt Evelyn's box. My eyes darted toward the front seat. Dad was focused on the road and Mom was complaining about their hotel bill in Italy. They weren't paying any attention to me.

I pictured all of my new nasturtium shoots and tried to remember how many had buds on them. There were tightly closed yellow buds. Could each one contain a topaz? Were there nuggets of agate inside the orange buds? Had the gem seed spell worked after all and was this a real baby ruby? I dragged my hand through my hair. For a half a second I wondered if I was leaving a priceless rainbow of emeralds, aquamarines, and sapphires behind.

Wait a minute.

Did Kat just fool me again? Was this a hoax? The baby ruby looked suspiciously like one of the red crystals from her witch's starter kit. Had Kat planted a fake gem for me to find? Maybe she was trying to make me believe in witchcraft so I'd come back next summer and be her friend again—and help her sell counterfeit jewels. I tapped my thumb on my leg, trying to figure it out.

Suddenly the books on Kat's shelf popped into my mind. *Sleight of Hand and How to Make Objects Disappear. Tabletop Magic. Chemicals that Change the Properties of Matter.* Then I pictured my dad mixing chemicals in his lab. His concoctions hissed and bubbled, sometimes changing colors.

I grabbed my iPhone and turned it on. Went to Amazon, clicked *books*, and typed in, "Chemicals that Change the Properties of Matter." Clicked on *Search inside this book* and read some random sentences. And my face got red hot.

"When magnesium reacts with oxygen the combination produces an extremely bright flame." I remembered the gem seed spell: *As I pictured the gem seed blossoming into a blue jewel, a fiercely bright spark shot out of the fifth hole.*

"Chemicals must dissolve in water before a reaction may take place."

"Before you drop in each seed, dip it into the charmed

water. It will help them to sprout. Ready?"

"How to create smoke using household ingredients like sugar…"

"By the power of sorcery, darkness, and the moon I name thee Topaz." The gem seed plunked into the third hole with a pinch of powdered finch claw. A wisp of smoke curled up and around them, escaping into the garden.

"They'll believe you, Sky, if you tell them the gems are legit. You're one of those trustworthy people. We can sell them, Sky. We're going to be wealthy as queens."

Alexa saw through Kat right away. I could still hear her giggling on the other end of the phone. "Oh my God, she really has you fooled!"

Maybe Kat *had* me fooled, but not anymore. As soon as we got home I could examine the gem under my dad's microscope. Maybe he'd help me do a chemistry experiment on the little red chip. Together we could figure out what it *really* was. I imagined my grandfather smiling and nodding his approval.

We turned off Pacific Coast Highway and I pulled out my cell and texted Alexa.

B hm n 5 min. Hv so much 2 tell u!

My cell jingled with Alexa's ring tone a second later.

Cl me asap! Dustn askd abt u agn! :)

My feet drummed against the floor with impatience. No way was I about to talk to Alexa about Dustin with my parents in the front seat. "Dad, why are you driving so *slow*?" I whined.

"Anxious to get home and talk to your friends?" he guessed.

My mom turned around and smiled at me. "You can

call your friends back in front of us," she teased. "Go ahead."

"That's OK. I want to unpack first." I eyed Evelyn's box, looking forward to sharing all the details of my summer with Alexa. And hearing what else Dustin Coles had asked about me. Did he want to know when I was coming home? Or if I had a boyfriend? It was amazing that the cutest boy in school had asked about me—*twice*. I could not wait to go to Pacific Middle School. Only two more weeks until school started and I would get to see Dustin again and find out if he really liked me.

As my dad pulled the car into the garage, I slid open the top of Evelyn's box and lifted the nasturtium with my index finger. Gently parting the petals, I stared at the tiny crystal that rested inside, and looked forward to solving the mystery of the gem seed spell.

Then I had the best idea yet: I could start my own detective agency! I could put an ad in the school paper and hang a sign on my door. My business cards would say: *The Skylar Robbins Detective Agency*, with my cell phone number and email address, and *No Case Too Large or Too Small*. I would have my cards printed just as soon as I solved this case. I could add, *Fluent in American Sign Language*, if I had learned it by then. Maybe somebody hearing-impaired would need my help.

"Hey Dad, after I unpack can I borrow your microscope?"

"If you use clean hands and don't move it off the table in the lab. Just be careful with it. What do you want to examine?" He opened the trunk and lifted out my suitcase.

"Just a flower. There's something growing in the middle of it that I really need to see up close."

I walked inside the house and hugged my mom again. Then I hurried to my room to unpack, my fingers tingling with anticipation. There was another adventure right around the corner. I could feel it. And this detective was ready to roll.

THE END

Skylar's adventures continue in

Skylar Robbins

The MYSTERY of the HIDDEN JEWELS

Turn the page for a sneak preview.

Contents

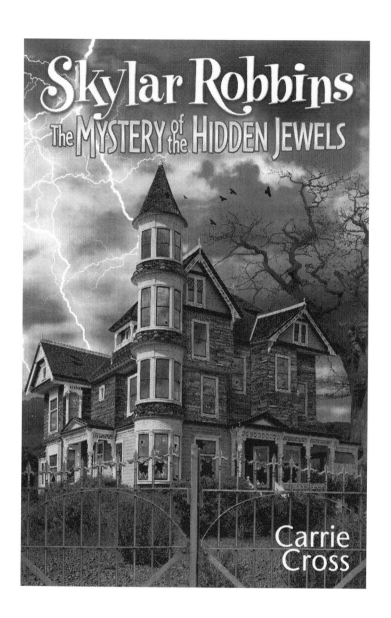

Introduction

Ididn't know this when I climbed into the backseat of the black Cadillac, but what was about to happen in the next half hour would change my life forever. And I'm not talking about a little change, either. This one was a monster. It wasn't just that we were moving out of the house I'd lived in since I was born, or that I was finally about to start middle school. Both of those things were huge, but they seemed like tiny details compared to what came next. The mystery I got tangled up in involved the disappearance of a famous heiress, a million dollars' worth of hidden jewels, and a threatening gang of bikers who were determined to find them before I did.

Could a skinny thirteen-year-old detective beat them to it?

You bet I could.

The first semester of middle school was anything but easy. By the time it was over I'd challenged the biggest bully in the entire seventh grade, kissed my first boy, and news of my detective agency had gone viral. Not to mention I risked my life to solve a mystery.

Again.

Psst! It's me, Skylar. Are you alone? I have something to tell you—but it's Top Secret. The Skylar Robbins Detective Agency needs a few Secret Agents to help solve my next case. I'm looking for special assistants to join me, undercover. But you must have mad detective skills. If you are right for the job, you will be able to answer these questions and post the answers on my website.

1. Decipher my web address and go to the site: moɔ.ƨniddoɿɿɒlyʞƨ.www

2. Find the Secret Agent Application Form.

3. Decode your secret password and enter it at the top of the form: 1-7-5-14-20

4. Select which fingerprint is mine: 1, 2, or 3.

1   2   3

5. Fill out the other important information.

When you complete these tasks, I'll email you an Identikit containing your Secret Agent ID and code name. I hope you will become one of my Secret Agents and help me solve the Mystery of the Hidden Jewels. I'll send you some free spy tips to get you started. See you in our next mystery!

Love, Skylar

Be on the lookout for these Skylar Robbins mysteries:
The Mystery of the Hidden Jewels
The Mystery of the Missing Heiress
The Curse of Koma Island

54456988R00146

Made in the USA
San Bernardino, CA
18 October 2017